THE
Prickleberry Pie
CONTEST

THE
Prickleberry Pie
CONTEST

KAREN GANGER

The Prickleberry Pie Contest

Copyright © 2021 by Karen Ganger. All rights reserved.

No part of this publication may be reproduced, stored in a retrieval system or transmitted in any way by any means, electronic, mechanical, photocopy, recording or otherwise without the prior permission of the author except as provided by USA copyright law.

The opinions expressed by the author are not necessarily those of URLink Print and Media.

1603 Capitol Ave., Suite 310 Cheyenne, Wyoming USA 82001
1-888-980-6523 | admin@urlinkpublishing.com

URLink Print and Media is committed to excellence in the publishing industry.

Book design copyright © 2021 by URLink Print and Media. All rights reserved.

Published in the United States of America

Library of Congress Control Number: 2021908369
ISBN 978-1-64753-785-2 (Paperback)
ISBN 978-1-64753-786-9 (Digital)

25.03.21

[1]

"WELL, THAT'S IT," CHARLEY SAID as his head scanned from left to right.

We stood together, side by side, holding hands, looking out across the sky and horizon. Before us stood a plain field, there was nothing in front of us except red clay scarred with circular grooves. Our toes stood on the edge of a concrete wall set into the soil, a huge cellar now open to the world and the elements. What happened to our beautiful trees? Our ancient oaks…gone…and my daffodils! My field of sunny yellow heirloom daffodils, that took years to naturalize now sent to kingdom come!" I choked. As I scanned the view all around us, there was absolutely no evidence of anything. Everything had been totally swept clean for miles.

"How could it be, Charley, that our home, its' contents, all the landscaping, all the shrubbery and the two hundred year old trees could just disappear like that?" I stood amazed. Even Charley's wine cellar in the basement of our home was now completely vacant. Not a shard of glass, not a drop of wine, not a stick of racking, nothing. It seemed as though a gigantic vacuum cleaner had sucked up everything and disappeared.

"I'm certainly glad we took off the whole week, ya' know. I would'a hated to see people get hurt or worse…" Charley's voice drifted off.

I stood there quiet, thinking. For eighteen years, Charley and I had owned and operated the Old Magnolia Plantation Bed & Breakfast in Cavanaugh, Mississippi. Originally built in the era before the Civil War, it was well maintained, eventually being registered in Mississippi's Historical Register. We welcomed the kind folk that had travelled worldwide to partake and share in our comfortable lodging and experience Southern hospitality at its' finest. Yes, we offered the best food anywhere in our region. Charley and I had made a good living, enjoyed the ambience, the lifestyle, the perks of owning and offering a true Southern specialty, and the beauty of our lovely home and town. Now it was gone.

We stood side-by-side each thinking private thoughts. I remembered when we first arrived here. We were so blind in love and the promise of a new venture was so exciting, we could hardly stand it without exploding in joy and laughter. Charley was such a wonderful chef when I first met him in New York. I had just graduated from the university in hotel management. Charley had just been awarded his second star. Soon, the business partners had a falling out. The economy took a downturn and Charley decided it was time to return to his roots. We moved to Cavanaugh shortly thereafter. I distinctly remember the day we purchased the Old Magnolia. Ah, the memories…

Every year, we closed Old Magnolia to the guests for a week during the Easter season so that we could refurbish our souls and relax. We always tried to do things that we had little time for when we had guests at the B&B. Sometimes, we would pretend that we were English aristocracy earlier in the century. Dress in whites, he in classic white linens, me in a long frilly dress with a sinfully large hat. Play a few sets of tennis, sit in a few garden chairs and sip on Pimm's Cups, wishing we could watch a polo match and entertain other guests at the B&B. This was just a little imaginary play in which to enjoy the company of each other. We could take some time and enjoy a few fantasies not otherwise indulged during the rest of the year. It was easy to romanticize every time I looked into his face. His piercing blue eyes and dark hair captured my heart. Most of the time, Charley was so finicky about the quality of food and so focused on the business, he would not enjoy himself otherwise taking time just for us or himself. It was time to forget about work. This week started out as just like all the other personal weeks we occasionally had for ourselves. Today, we decided to see an adventure film. Something we rarely treated ourselves to. I guess, in looking at it now, we could have stayed home for a real adventure, but then again, our safety comes to mind. In the end, to question whether we were upset, no. To feel beaten, no. Indifferent, maybe somewhat. This had been our third tornado in seven years. There was no grief this time around. We had lost all our heirlooms, all our special things, our sentimental belongings in the first. From the second, we lost the replacements. We had started a family here, then lost our little boy by terminal disease. There was too much heartbreak in Cavanaugh to stay now. This time, it didn't matter anymore, personal belongings were not so important. We had each other, that is what really counted. It was time to move on.

"Third time's a charm, kiddo!" Charley grinned and squeezed my hand.

"Strike out!" I exclaimed.

"Let's go," he said and he spun us around away from the large gaping hole in the earth. My feet seemed to rotate while in place.

With that and nothing more, we turned and walked back to the car. No place to go, no need to pack, no destination, no plan. Charley started the engine and backed up. He was going to pull out onto the road, forward, with our backs to a now distant past.

"Stop!" I yelled and exited the vehicle. "One miracle!"

Our beautiful sign, "The Old Magnolia Plantation" still inscribed and painted from old carved cedar, stood near the roadside. The only item left on our property stood, stabbed with a pitchfork strewn from the sky. On the top of the impaled pitchfork, a white cloth fluttered in the breeze. Walking over to it, I wondered, was this some sort of sign? A white flag of surrender, perhaps? A Buddhist prayer flag, for peace? I yanked it off and carried it back to the car. I jumped back in and shut the door. Charley was ready to pull out onto the road.

"What is it?" He asked.

"I wouldn't want our friends and neighbors to see this." I said, breaking into giggles. "I especially wouldn't want anyone to think they were mine!"

Holding up the white cloth with both hands, we both looked at a large pair of granny's panties. Yep, I could hear the comments for years…

"She lost everything but her shorts!"

The wheels spun on the gravel as they hit the asphalt road and we headed west.

[2]

WELL, TO MAKE A LONG story short, we ended up in Silent Springs, Arkansas. It was a sleepy little burg in the Ozarks that had seen better days. Don't misunderstand me, potentially, it had a little charm but the ambience had deserted it a long time ago. When Charley and I arrived, the downtown consisted of a post office, a café, a church and an antiques shop surrounding a town square that could only qualify as a weed lot. Several stone buildings stood vacant in various stages of dilapidation. The town itself showed evidence that at least in the early nineteen-twenties it was an active vital community. The area itself had possessed a thriving apple growing industry and was known nationwide as growing the finest eating and cider apples in America. Then, like the Great Depression, the great freeze hit and damaged all the orchards and industry. No longer could one smell the sweet fragrance of apple blossoms or watch the light pink blossom petals dance on the breeze. As years went on, the local farmers turned to cattle and chicken ranching. Silent Springs was just a place now in which a small two lane highway passed through.

That afternoon, when Charley and I drove through, we could have missed it in a blink of an eye. In fact, we sped through then Charley braked, hung a bat turn and came back. There was something that caught his fancy. We pulled over and stepped out of the car. Yep, this was going to be the place, I thought. I could see that look in Charley's face.

"This place! Look at this place, Francine! Isn't this the greatest?" Charley looked possessed.

I could almost hear the wheels and gears clicking inside his head.

"Well, yes, Charley, it's cute." I lied. "It has a lot of potential. It would take a lot of work, and a community effort, but the town square could be really charming." I agreed but deep down, I had some hesitation. "We don't know anything about this place. Maybe the water tastes bad, maybe they have crime, maybe…"

"Francine, stop being a weak Wilma and help me dream here. I like this place." He had made a decision. There was no going back now. His decision was for the both of us. No arguing. Knowing Charley, I had to accept it. At that moment, we both knew in our hearts that this small town would be our life goal.

We would rebuild our lives and refurbish this little hamlet to something, well not exquisite, but the type of place you wanted to be, all the time.

"Welcome home, Francine!" Charley looked over at me and smiled.

We drove around the area and looked around. Just to the west of the town square and down the street about three-quarters of a mile, sat a lovely quiet lake of the same name. Silent Springs Lake was situated on a beautiful natural setting that drew in the wildlife. Beside an inlet on the lake stood a small ice packing plant, the Silent Springs Ice Company, still drawing up the fresh tasty cold spring water and freezing it into sparkling diamond shaped cubes. Outside of that, there did not appear to be any commercial industry for nearly thirty miles.

Charley and I first rented a small cottage near the lake and then set our sights on downtown. After much hassle, we eventually were successful in acquiring the largest vacant building to support a new venture, Silent Springs Grocery – Purveyors of Fine Fresh Food.

Since we were newcomers to this area, we had our doubts about being accepted by the local residents. After all, this was a small town, a close knit community. A lot of people in this neck of the woods would be hesitant to befriend outsiders. We'd give it the old college try. What could be more necessary or accessible than a grocery store? As our financial investment began to show in our grocery store improvements, people took notice. We tried to introduce ourselves to the locals at the café and were always acknowledged as the "new folks".

"We can either sink or swim, darlin', on this one," Charley always remarked.

I was afraid that most of these folks, being so isolated from the big city, would not accept us, our eclectic food variety. Maybe they were just the standard meat and potato people. To draw the interest and get participation from our new community, Charley had his winning ways. Boy, could he be persuasive! The real saving grace was visiting every residence in a ten mile radius and get commitments from nearly everyone. Local produce, local goods, locals to buy and sell our merchandise. Finally, a market close to home for these folks. Why, we'd sell the freshest milk, butter and cheese, eggs, various meats and produce that tasted like they were supposed to. Who wouldn't want to bite into a fresh crisp apple or juicy sunny warm summer peach? A fresh summer tomato salad with scallions and basil from Aunt Martha's garden, doesn't that sound utterly delicious to you? And Charley? He was still in his glory baking fresh breads, biscuits, cinnamon rolls and other goodies for sale every morning. Those travelers that never blinked as they passed on the highway now could not resist the fragrant aromas wafting into their autos and trucks. It seemed everyone stopped in now. When we expanded into offering fresh sandwiches, chips and sodas, Lou and Kathy Evans at the Chuckwagon Café were a little miffed. Just a little explanation that we cannot compete with their wonderful entries, our sandwich offerings were really designed for the road. Our customers were for those folks en route to picnics, work, traveling on down the road. We were not trying to take their business, not even compete with them. To prove it, we showed them how we wrapped each sandwich and "brown-bagged" the lunch menu. The only place to nosh was in the customer's car. Well, that was OK then and we became close friends.

Our business took off and serviced the general area. We were small though, and our selections were limited. Some people called us "chi-chi" for offering eclectic coffee, scones and other city folk fare, but generally, we were now part of the town and had a steady loyal clientele. The sausage biscuit morning crowd would have to stay at the Chuckwagon Café. We didn't want to horn in on the Evans' livelihood. We didn't want to steal their customers either but we did need to offer food that customers wanted. Highway travelers always stopped for purchases but it seemed that there was still hesitation with customers. Our town just did not have the charm to draw more people. If a family came in to stop for a couple of sandwiches, they just didn't want to stay. It seemed as if they wanted to run back to the car and drive off quickly. We were both concerned and began some self-searching for an answer and a solution, though neither one of us said anything to each other. Life continued on and the calendar clicked away.

[3]

WE HAD BEEN WELCOMED WHOLE-HEARTEDLY into Silent Springs and this truly became our home. After a few years, everyone knew Charley and everyone liked him. He evolved into being our honorary mayor. As for me, I'm too shy. I've never been as outgoing as Charley and I probably never will but I do my best to be friendly and helpful and warm and thoughtful and sincere. Despite our efforts, Silent Springs experienced no growth. The downtown square still remained a weed lot and no new businesses came to fill in the vacant stone buildings I viewed every day. Looking at them, I could see a bright future here, but who, who would come and fill them, and bring life?

"Charley", I told him one day, "no one comes here because the town square looks like a dump."

We both looked out of the window into the town square. It was nothing more than a weed-filled lot with a lot of wind-blown trash lying about. A crow stood perched on a large dead branch of some long gone arborial volunteer. It let out a raucous caw, reminding us of some Hitchcock thriller.

"I've been thinking about this for a long time. We don't draw as many customers as we should because they are afraid. Are we just a bump in the road? Are we just a sleezy place? I don't rightfully know, but I think we need to do something about this. Charley, we have an investment to protect and nourish!"

"Francine, I've thought about it a lot too. In fact, I'm throwing a town meeting next Tuesday night here."

"You mean in the store?" I asked.

"Yep. I've sent word out. Let's just see what happens. Francine, I know we've been happy here. Would we have done something different? Yes, probably so, but I think as I did on Day One, that we could alter this town into something really great. We've brought a lot with us and we've done a lot but I've been disappointed that no one has come to share this with us".

"I know, Charley, I know. I feel the same way." I admitted.

It was true. Now that Charley had an idea and didn't really share it with me, still was not a problem. He'll let me know before the rest of the town, I was sure of that. At night, we talked about needing a moneymaker. As a community, we needed to raise money. How do you do that when the local population seems to have no interest in doing anything to improve their town? A lot of our citizens were just too busy trying to squeek by and make a living. Too many of them ran a livestock business and still commuted elsewhere to a second job to keep up with financial demands. The wheels in Charley's head were moving, gearing up and down. It was fun watching him thinking how to fix up Silent Springs.

He started having town meetings every Tuesday night in the store after closing time. Everyone that showed up still looked to grab a free cookie or cup of coffee. Well, if that was the way to entice them so be it. The meetings started slow, then like a snowball heading downhill, it built up speed. Jeter Davis, who owned the garage and towing service on the edge of town, suggested that we appoint a police officer.

"We could nail tourists and travelers for speed. Write 'em tickets! Big ones! We'll use the money to fix up our square." Jeter offered.

Mertie Kramer argued back, "Are you dense, Mister? We want people to love our town, not hate it. Who's goin' to pay an officer's salary anyway? We don't have any money as it is. What are you thinkin'? How many people'll want to come here if they figure out we're a speed trap?"

Chester Kramer, Mertie's husband, knew her blood pressure was starting to rise. He tapped her arm. "Now dear, let's not get fired up here. We're just havin' a brain-storming session, is all." He brushed her gray hair away from her face and they sat down.

"That's right!" Several participants chanted together.

THE PRICKLEBERRY PIE CONTEST

After nearly an hour, Charley poured himself another cup of coffee from the urn on the counter. It was getting too difficult to have town meeting in the grocery store. Not enough seating to go around for everyone now. The idea that meetings should be held at the Chuckwagon Café seemed more sensible. There was more room for seating there but somehow Charley couldn't break from the control and hold his meetings elsewhere.

"OK, then," Charley started. "I don't want anybody to ask questions, ya'll just have to trust me on this. But, I have a plan!"

He then proceeded to ask everyone and he meant everyone in town, to put out the word. Everyone was to meet in the town square on Saturday at eight in the morning. Split those perennials, bring some flower bulbs, seedlings, bushes, saplings, plant volunteers, brick, stone, extra lumber, garden tools and hardware. We need manpower. We need womanpower, kidpower, boy-scouts, girl-scouts, FFA! Move it, move it, move it! I was getting tired just listening to him. More amazing was the fact that my husband had materialized a whole town as a work force.

On Saturday morning, surprisingly, nearly one hundred and fifty people showed up. Rance Waite drove his tractor over to the square and worked diligently digging a small fish pond. He helped grade and smooth everything. Steve Kyper, son of the lumber yard owner, drove in a flat bed truck with plenty of lumber, cement and other building supplies. Someone brought wrought iron fence sections. The whole square buzzed with activity. Even the State Police stopped to find out what all the hubbub was about. From the grocery store window, I watched a county sheriff exit his patrol car and actually pick up a shovel and help somebody plant a tree. Brickwork was being laid and stone benches were made. A beautiful gazebo was built. Pathways led to a lawn area, flower beds planted, a water fountain sang with the sound of tinkling water drops. It truly was lovely and all constructed off a diagram Charley had doodled the night before. In the late afternoon, only the diehards were left there to clean up. All day long, the customers ran in and out. The chiller was empty of sodas and bottled water. The shelves were emptied of chips and cookies and other goodies that produced enough energy to keep going. All the day-workers seemed to have cleaned out the stock. I kept trying, as a good neighbor to offer free drinks and snacks, but they kept coming. Our sales today were going to be through the roof. Looking out the grocery store window into the square, I could stare in amazement. It was gorgeous.

"OK, Charley!" I heard someone yell in the darkening sky. "Now what?"

"Yeah, Charley, what's yer plan? We've been here all day waitin' for your answer." Someone else asked him.

"That, my friends, is for you to find out. See you Tuesday night." Charley answered.

"Aw, that's not fair," came the voice again.

"Oh yes, it is! Just wait." Charley yelled back as he walked to his truck in the dark. I watched the others disburse somewhat dejectedly.

"He ain't got no plans, Jarvis." The voice came again.

"Oh yes I do, Loyal! Hey, I can't tell you when I haven't even told my wife yet." I saw Charley's head turn towards the window and saw his bright smile through the deep darkness. "Dang!"

[4]

ON MONDAY NIGHT AFTER WE closed the grocery, Charley and I strolled through the town square. We marveled at the accomplishment. The work party had turned out better than our wildest imagination or expectation. It seemed the excitement was now contagious. People were talking about how wonderful it was. Somebody suggested that we have an opening ceremony. A news crew stopped by today and filmed a segment for tonights' newscast. There was still a lot to do in our town, but it was a definite improvement. If only we could draw some business owners to move in. The majority of downtown buildings were still vacant. More so, should I say dilapidated. These buildings need a lot of work. Who would want to invest in a dead town? Were we foolish enough to think that we could help rebuild a town or chasing a dream? As we walked home, holding hands, I stopped for just a second and tossed a penny in the water fountain.

"I just made a wish, Charley!"

"I know, honey." Charley answered as he squeezed my hand.

We walked the few blocks home in the dark. The air was cool and there was a light breeze from the south. As I entered the house, I headed straight for the living room sofa. I plopped down and kicked off my shoes. My feet hurt. I felt tired.

"Hey, hon?" Charley yelled from the kitchen.

"Yes, my man." I answered, knowing full well he was going to ask me to get up and do something for him. I knew it because I was so dog tired. My feet scooted around the floor feeling for my shoes.

"Don't let me forget to take the letters with me tomorrow. I do not want to mail them from our Post Office. I cannot afford those nosy snoops and busybodies to discover our surprise!"

"OK", I answered. I stood up slipping my feet into my shoes.

"While I'm thinkin' about it, would you go put those letters on the front seat of my truck?"

And there it was, his instruction. "Can't a girl get any rest around this place?" I laughed and moved towards the entry hall where the letters sat on the table. I snatched them up and opened the front door wondering if the truck was actually there in the garage or not. I couldn't remember if he parked in the driveway or parked it in the garage yesterday. It was nice to live in a place where you could walk to work and not drive everywhere. My mind was wandering. When I returned from the garage, I found that Charley had poured us each a nice glass of wine. A platter sat on the coffee table with crackers, cheese and wonderfully fragrant sliced ripe pear.

"Yum!" I said as I kicked off my shoes for a second time and started walking towards him.

Charley raised his eyebrows twice, his secret message to me. Then he patted the sofa cushion inviting me to sit beside him. We both raised our glasses and clinked them together. "Chin-chin!" What a wonderful way to end the day.

[5]

IT WAS TUESDAY AND WE were so busy at the store it was hard to keep up with the orders. Customers seemed to swarm into the grocery all day. While Charley was working the bakery and drinks section, I was working the sandwich deli and regular groceries. I couldn't put my finger on it. It was not my imagination that there was a buzz in the air. When we had a break in activity and the store emptied out, I leaned against the counter. Charley was wiping off the espresso machine.

"Something's up," I said.

"You noticed that too? At first I thought it was just me. At one point I saw Verle Perkins walk in. I thought, OK. But when Alma Periwinkle came in, that cut it. "Something's goin' on." Charley announced.

"And you know what, Charley? Alma Periwinkle spent fifty-two dollars and thirty-four cents in here!"

"She didn't!" Charley exclaimed.

"She did!" I answered.

"Why that ole gal just loosened up her purse strings. Hell, she can't hardly let go of a dollar bill she puts in the collection plate at church!"

"I know it!"

"Francine, what did she buy? I haveta' know…"

Just then another couple of customers walked in and we stopped the gossip talk. Funny, how we sounded just like a pair of cackling hens. We have always closed by six-thirty every evening. Charley always said that if you didn't have your fresh dinner ingredients by that time at night, it was too late to cook. It was closing time and we still had a store full of people. After the day we've had, I had no more energy. I honestly didn't know if I could stay for the community meeting. I was so tired.

Charley was talking to several men and putting the finishing touches on getting the coffee urn up and running at the same time. Without stopping a moment, he started getting a plate of a new variety of cookies arranged. He had experimented with them yesterday. I guess he was using his buddies at the meeting as guinea pigs. Once he glanced over to the platter, he realized he'd better wait a while to put it out. It seemed like the men were a bunch of wolves ready to devour anything that was put in front of them. If the platter of cookies were set out now, they would disappear by the time the meeting started. The store continued to fill up and space was really becoming an issue. I started removing goods from the counters and placing them in the back room. Having cleaned the counters, people started to sit on them and wait for the meeting to begin. Boy, this was going to be a doozy.

By meeting time, it was standing room only. Most of the crowd was comprised of friends or friendly faces we'd seen before, however, there were a lot of new people. They looked like kindly folk, locals who now had an interest in their own backyard. Oh Lord, I spied a girl standing posed with a pen in one hand and a shorthand notebook in the other.

"Are you a reporter?" I asked her.

"No'm, ah'm not". She drawled.

"Oh." I half said out loud.

"Naw, Ah'm Peggy Elkin's daughter. She tole me to come on down here and take notes 'cuz she cain't miss anything, ya know. She stepped on a wasp today and her foot is mighty swole up". Her response fired off faster than a machine gun in heat.

"I'm so sorry to hear that," I answered. "Please tell her that we hope she feels better soon, Miss…Miss Elkins…"

"Oh sorry… I'm Ruta. Well, my name is Ruta Mae. But ah don't like the Mae part. It's too ole-fashioned."

Poor Ruta, I thought. She just kept firing off more conversation than I wanted to hear. The girl just rambled on and on. Before I knew it, I realized that the meeting had started. Glancing over to

Charley, he looked pained. How would he fend off the dogs? He clearly didn't want to give away his secrets yet.

"Thanks everybody! I really mean thanks to everybody. Well, I hope you are all here today. I'd certainly hate to leave any thanks gone unnoticed, you know what I mean. We had a mighty fine turnout this last weekend. It was more than I could have imagined. Hey, let's give everyone a hand!" Charley started his schtick.

The crowd was evidently pleased with themselves. A roaring cheer rose up.

"Now, I have to say that the work was phenomenal. You all accomplished so much! Our town square is, well… well… just bea-you-ti-full! I'm nearly speechless! Let's give each other a hand for that!"

The crowd again clapped and whistled. Guys were patting each other on the back and shoulder. Now I thought, the Master will show how skillful he really is. Everyone is chomping at the bit to find out what the next step is. How will he skirt that? I wondered.

Charley continued, "I don't have enough time or enough hot air to thank all of you individually".

A chuckle rose up.

"So what I'd like everybody to do is to individually give us your name and tell us what you worked on. What, if anything, inspired you. What you brought or donated and how your individual project developed. Let's start here with Steve. Steve?" Charley's head nodded to Steve Kyper while his arm flung out showing the direction of the next speakers.

Ah, the master stroke, I thought.

"Uh, hi! I'm Steve Kyper. Uh, I didn't know I'd have to say something but…"and on it went.

Kudos to Charley. He knew how to manipulate without them realizing it. Roughly forty-five minutes later, the last speaker finished his piece. Charley stood up then.

"Is there anybody we missed? Is there anyone that you worked with last weekend that is not here tonight?" A few people shouted names.

"Please, when you see them, tell them how much we appreciated their help. Our town square is the prettiest, prettiest square, just, well, anywhere. Frankly, I can't think of one better'n ours. Whatcha all think?" Again, the crowd clapped and cheered.

"I am so humbled by y'all. I am so proud of y'all. I'm just overwhelmed. I want to tell you 'Welcome Home". This is your place and y'all should be proud." Charley continued to pour on the charm. "I've made this town my home and I will remain here in Silent Springs 'til my dyin' days and then some. Yeah, that's right. I'm never leavin'…too beautiful. The folks here are the finest a man could know. Hey Ted, that reminds me. We need to talk about a little plot over at the cemetery."

The crowd gave a few chuckles and smiled. I thought to myself, when did my husband change himself into this ultra politician, oh brother!

"Well", he continued, "I know y'all came on down here tonight to hear me tell all of you my plan. And honestly, I'd like to".

"Yeah, yeah, Charley!" Several town folk chanted.

"But right now, I can't. Believe me! I need y'all to trust me. I will do it soon and I will do it big, but the time is not right, we have to wait".

"But, but, but. Is that all we get from you, Charley Simson? Hot butt gas?" Pete Snow snickered.

The crowd shook their heads in agreement.

"Now listen…please! I've contacted some people about our project. Folks, this is OUR project. Not just mine. It's OURS! And since it's ours, we have to do it right. Understand?"

"Ah-ha!" I said to myself. Here's the part on ownership. He'll sell everybody and make them believe it is their plan, when all along it is his and only his. I chuckled under my breath.

"This is the deal…" Charley continued. "I've contacted several people. Several famous people…"

"Oooohhhh!" The crowd chimed in together.

"I can't tell y'all who all will be here yet until I get their confirmations. Now, it won't take long. Just bear with me a few weeks. Can y'all do that?" Everyone shook their heads in an affirmative manner.

"Now…does anyone have anything else to say?" Charley asked in a somewhat miffed tone.

Everyone looked around the room and at each other, then shakily, Ivy Miller's arm went up. A shushing sound came up. Somebody yelled "Let her speak" and all eyes fell on Ivy, who kept her head down. Poor Ivy, her timidity preceded her. She was the epitome of so many country wives, isolated by the sheer countryside and responsibility of running a home and a farm. She worked hard at home and raising a large family. She kept her house sparkling clean, and the yard was neat and clean, a picture perfect model for Farm Today. She was active in the church, and was known as a true craftsman for fine quality quilts.

"Well", she mumbled, "with y'alls work so hard last weekend, I ha'nt seen the square so alive, at least since I was a little girl. I said to Loyal, my husband Loyal, that somethin' here is takin' place and I want to be part of it. Now, y'all know my daughter Suzanna received a nice settlement when her Myles was taken so tragically. An' nobody never said a thing. She said to me 'Mama, I got that money in the bank to he'p you'. I tole my chile that that money was compensation for her baby an' an' she tole me that no amount of money can replace Myles, who was kilt. But I tell you this, she said, 'Mama, this town has been good to us. Nobody said anything to us. Nobody asked us for money, about money, nothing. Everyone here in Silent Springs let us grieve and let us wear ourselves away from the horror and tragedy. We have appreciated this to no end'. It's time to give back. So, to y'all, we're investin' in this here town. Today, I signed a lease. My daughter Suzanna and I are opening the Quiltin' Bee Shop. We'll be sellin' our quilts, sewn goods and givin' lessons. I hope y'all come and make the endeavor a success. I thank ya".

With that, Ivy sat down and moved her head downwards staring at her shoes. The crowd then clapped and cheered, "Ivy, Ivy, Ivy!" So there it was, the most unpretentious woman in town, taking a stand and a move in a positive manner.

Hallelujah, I whispered to myself, with tears building, our town is starting to grow.

[6]

NEARLY A MONTH AND A half passed by. Ivy Miller's Quilting Bee was opened and surprisingly did a smashing business. Most of her inventory snapped up so quickly, the poor woman was working day and night trying to re-supply her shop and fill orders.

Peggy and Ty Elkins followed up and just celebrated their grand opening of Buds and Blooms Flower Shop located next to the Quilting Bee. Peggy certainly has a talent in flower arranging, but to me, the most amazing transformation is the décor and Ruta Mae, who has found a niche as a talented arranger. Why the shop outside is so pretty, it reminds me of the flower market in Paris.

Little by little, Silent Springs looks better everyday. Business has been so steady and increasing, Charley and I have expanded, packing full lunches for fisherman and day-trippers at the lake. Just yesterday while Charley prepared a prosciutto and fontina pannini, his customer mentioned he was here opening a pharmacy at the other end of town square. Charley invited him to our meeting offering to introduce him to our friendly folks.

"Good evenin', folks!" Charley announced. Greetings went 'round the room.

"I'd like y'all to meet Joe Fonte. Joe here is openin' Joe's Old Fashioned Pharmacy in the old accountant's office space. Say hello to Joe!"

Everybody just like in school repeated, "Hello, Joe!"

"Well, I guess that's new business. Please introduce yourselves to Joe after the meetin' and offer your lip should he need some" Charley said. "Now, I know y'all have been waitin; a long long time to hear somethin' and tonight is the night!"

THE PRICKLEBERRY PIE CONTEST

Everybody sat intently watching Charley. So attentive were they that I'd rightly felt they were hearing about this plan for the very first time.

"As y'all know, I've told you folks that I have a plan for our town. I don't know how y'all will feel about it, whether y'all want to participate in it but, hey, we've come so far now, we can't let this slip by. Look what we've accomplished with the town square. See'n that so many of you have invested your time, your money an' all. Ivy… Peggy and Ty…Whitey… Charley looked at Whitey Snow who had owned the ramshackle Highway Café across the street. Whitey has spruced up his place to the point where there is usually an hour's wait every weekend to get seated at a table. Good thing the Chuckwagon is now open for lunch and dinner only because Whitey's Highway Café would be givin' them a run for their breakfast money, hah!

Initially, I had a desire to improve our town by creating an opportunity to raise funds. These funds would be used to spruce up the buildings, the businesses, the square, the park and other things in general.

First of all, before I tell you HOW we will accomplish this, I must inform y'all that we need to legitimize our activities. We need to set up a committee, a city council per se. It will be the responsibility of the committee to assure the funds will be managed appropriately. I can't do it all myself nor do I want to. We will need to set up a town election. We need Herb Larsen here to draw up a charter. And Bob Perkins at Silent Springs Bank, we'll need him to set up an account to hold our funds. We can earn interest on money we've developed as a town."

Charley went on and on with the details. Somewhere in the back of my mind, I heard him drone on with uninteresting details, which I later regretted, but at the time, all I could do was to fight against dozing off. I finally lost the battle, my head tucked down onto my chest. Sitting on the floor behind the counter with my back propped up against the door frame to the back storage room, I awoke to yelling and cheers.

"Minnie Pearl, can you imagine that?" I heard someone say.

"Julia Child, why, she's the French chef on TV! And James Beard! He's known at the father of American Cooking. He's a real luminary!"

"Yeah, but Irma Bombeck, she's the best. She is my favorite. My, she is the funniest woman alive. Wow, this is terrific!"

As I stood up and dusted myself off, I could see the whole town received the message. It was like fireworks going off. Charley was beaming, his hand was being pumped like a top politician. He was a true hero in their eyes. The townfolk took a lot of time leaving tonight. I tried to straighten up the store but I was seriously still so tired, I actually felt as if I had been drugged. My actions were strictly on automatic. At one point, I heard Charley say,

"Francine, here honey, leave that for me."

He touched my arm to stop me from wiping off a table.

"Here, let me do that."

"No, that's OK, I'll do it. You've had a big night, just let me finish here."

He grabbed my arm forcing me to stop and told me, "Let me do it."

I was so tired. I just didn't have the energy to argue.

"Charley, I'm so tired. I can't seem to wake up enough to get the shop ready for tomorrow." I suddenly felt hot.

"Honey," he said as he gave me a big squeezy bear hug, "That's OK. Just go on home. I'll handle it. Hey, do you want me to walk you home or have somebody take you? France, I'm so pumped I couldn't go and stay home now to relax even if I wanted to, I'll clean and lock up."

"It's OK," I said. "I can get myself home. Love you."

"Love you too, babe." Charley said as he bent over for a quick kiss.

I stepped out of the store and realized the truck was parked outside. I jumped in and started to head home. I felt glad that we hadn't walked to work today. There was a comfort in getting behind the wheel and just sitting there. Somehow, the breeze felt good and I suddenly felt alive. I smiled as the ignition cranked over and put it into gear.

[7]

THE FOLLOWING MORNING, CHARLEY AND I had a wonderful breakfast. Both rested and feeling perky, conversation just seemed to flow. For some reason, the coffee tasted really good.

"Charley?" I asked quizzically. "I've been thinking this morning. I need to make a doctor's appointment. I think it's been a while since I've last gone. I've been so tired lately. I can't scrounge up enough energy to keep up with you."

"Honey, you and I have both been pretty busy lately. Things are not going to slow down for a long while. Yes, go."

"I know. That's why I'm so worried. I don't know why I have such fatigue and I really want to help you. Despite being so tired, I don't think I'm sleeping too well". I said, wiping my forehead, "Whew, it's hot in here."

Charley turned around with a slight smile on his face. Then his expression changed. "My gosh, Francine, let me deal with all this. It's my project. I haven't asked you for any help."

"But Charley," I said guiltily, "We're a team. Everybody in this town sees us as a team, a pair, a couple. If they don't see me working with you on this, they'll all say 'What's the matter with her?' I can't have that."

"Oh, hon. I understand. You'll be there with me and you'll be there for me, Francine."

Deep down though, I felt that Charley was seeing some overreaction on my part. Worrying about being tired. How crazy was that? Was I being irrational? Well, things go through your mind, especially when you lose a child. It's something that a mother can never really get over. I've repressed a lot of memory and grief. I just never could talk to Charley about it. Losing our little Kit almost killed me. The death of my mother months before and dealing with a two year old dying of a rare blood cancer, of losing your home by a tornado a year later, there was just too much to swallow for a while. It would have been easier if Mother was still alive when Kit was sick. Somebody to talk to or help me cope would have helped. Faith got me through and our Pastor helped but it was the worst experience of my life regardless. I keep up a good face because I don't want Charley to worry. I sometimes think that it bothers him too. But he's a man and he never learned to talk about things like that either. Sometimes, I think that is why we care so much for each other. We have to be close for each other. Silence on loss keeps the hurt inside in a deep-down pocket and so we don't bother each other with it. He probably thinks I think I have a rare blood cancer, I know I don't but I just don't feel right.

We both grabbed our personal stuff and the money bag and walked out of the house. Another day at the store. Actually, I was excited about creating a new pasta salad I could serve with our sandwiches. A little lagniappe, a little extra. Something different from the usual macaroni salad or potato salad. I've spent a lot of time perfecting this new recipe and today I intend to make a batch and watch for the results. Of course, Charley is still the chef, however I want a little more experience creating and selling food, not just selling the regular groceries. Who knows, maybe I'll start a catering business some day.

"By the way, Big C, I found a new vendor I'd like to contact today. Italian Specialties, how about that?" I asked.

"Francine, it sounds lovely. But what kinds? Refrigerated meat and cheese or bottles and jars?" He inquired.

"Bottles and jars. Olives, caponata, pesto, marinara, stuff like that. I've thought a lot about this, Charley, and I think we should expand, offering gourmet exotica. Nobody sells imported foods here for fifty miles. Wouldn't it be great to cut a big slab of panettone?"

"Yeah," Charley agreed as he unlocked the store door. "Actually, it would be fantabulous! Christmas time would be awesome. Sometimes I miss Little Italy.

Ah, it'd be heaven to go to New York City just for a bite of great Italian food."

"Ooooohhh, German zimsterne, lebkuchen, pfeffernusse, oh Charley, that is!"

"Is what," Charley asked.

"Awesome, you big goof!" I turned and gave him a kiss. "Now let's get busy."

The morning went so smoothly, the routine was down pat. After a while, Charley sat in the back room working on details, made a few phone calls and wrote in his project manager. For the life of me, I have no idea how any of this could take so long. How much planning did he need to do anyway? After the lunch rush when we hit a slow spot, I left him at the store and ran off to Dr. Wiggin's office. I must have been gone only about an hour and a half. When I returned, I spied a huge banner strung out across the front of the town square.

Actually, it was not hard to miss. Anyone traveling on the highway would see it. In bright red letters, the banner read,

"Welcome to Silent Springs first annual Prickleberry Pie Contest!

August 1st – Celebrities, Pie Contest, Games, Fun – Silent Springs Square"

There on the square a large purple box fashioned like a giant blackberry fixed to a pole stood the entry box. There were instructions stapled to the wooden post and entry forms. I noticed several people starting to congregate in the square when I jumped out of the truck.

"Sorry, dear!" I heard Mrs. Wimbledon say to me.

"Oh yes, terribly sorry of me. This took me by surprise." I apologized. In my excitement jumping out of the truck, I had bumped into her.

"Took you by surprise, dear?" she asked. "Why'd I thought you knew all about this, married to Charley and all..."

"Well, yes, no, sort of." I laughed. "I'm quite sorry, Mrs. Wimbledon. I don't know what to say. What I mean to say is that, yes, this was coming, but...I wasn't ready for it. Well, I am but it came as a shock. Oh, not a shock, a...a... a... oh I don't know. I'm at a loss for words, sorry." I just kept babbling nonstop.

"Francine, you may call me Pamela. Honey, you look as if you'd just seen a ghost."

"Mrs. Wimbledon, uh, Pamela, the truth is that I just returned from Dr. Wiggins' office and I am pre-occupied. Sorry again. I am just rambling."

"Francine, is everything alright?" she asked in such sincerity. The little English lady in the middle of the deep south Ozarks, so funny, why is she actually here? She put her arm around me and helped walk me into the grocery.

"Yes, actually I'm fine. I guess I've been so busy with all this stuff lately I wasn't paying attention to my female vibes, you know what I'm talking about? You know a lady knows when something is wrong? That kind of thing."

"So is something wrong, dear? Pamela asked.

""Well, no, not really. I just found out that I'm going into menopause. I never really thought about it and I think deep down, I always thought that maybe I'd have another child. Now I know I won't."

She turned to look me in the face, "I didn't know you had children, you and Charley."

"We don't anymore, we lost our Kit when he was a two year old. He died of a blood cancer similar to leukemia. We've been brokenhearted ever since. Please, please do not say anything to anyone. No one knows what we have had to face before moving here. I can't have Charley thinking about the past right now when he has so much on his mind. Actually I don't even know why I just told you". I sunk down into a chair and Pamela patted my shoulder.

"We must go on, nothing said. Now, can I get a couple tuna salad sandwiches and some tea cookies? My bridge club is tonight and it's my turn to entertain."

"That is not a problem, Pamela." I responded as I lifted myself out of the chair. "In fact, let me do this for you. I have some small cutters I've been dying to try out. They are card shapes, clubs, spades, hearts and diamonds. How would that work? You can take them home and try them out. With the cut sandwiches, dip the sides in chopped parsley or paprika or whatever you desire. By the way, I didn't know you had a bridge club here in Silent Springs."

"Now that would be lovely, Francine. And yes we do. I started a bridge club after I moved here. Had to have a little bit of home, you know. We keep it quiet. We can't have too many farm wives involved and drawn away from their work. The men would get mad. Francine, don't worry, you'll be fine. But, could you indulge me one last question? Why, is the pie contest called Prickleberry? That's an unusual name."

"My husband, Charley, attributes it to a comment Julia Child made. She was in Paris and tasted something so wonderful she said it gave her prickles on her arms! She had never tasted anything quite like it. I guess that was one reason why she learned the art of French cooking. She needed to replicate what she loved eating."

I spent the rest of the afternoon in the shop working contentedly and surprisingly quite busy. I hadn't really talked to Charley since I returned from the doctor's office. Around three o'clock, we ran out of coffee and I put on a fresh pot. The fragrance of the fresh brew really woke me up. I saw Charley talking to a number of people in the square. I hadn't even realized that he was not in the shop with me. Suddenly, it occurred to me that I was hungry. Hungry for a little pizza. But how? Charley had been so pre-occupied with today's prickleberry pie contest planning he's neglected his duties. I found a large bowl of bread dough proofing and rolled some out to make a pizza. I smoothed out some olive oil onto a large baking sheet, opened a jar of Italian marinara sauce, popped some olives on it, fresh basil, sliced onions, fresh tomatoes from my lunch set-ups, I sprinkled some parmesan and mozzarella on it and baked it until it was golden and bubbly. I cut the whole tray into three inch squares.

Then I wrote on a small chalkboard, "Hot Pizza Bites Now Out of the Oven 2/$1" and flipped the chalkboard to show on the square. Obviously, the fragrance was overpowering and people seemed to run into the shop, including Charley.

"Oh my gosh, honey! This is perfect! I was trying to figure out where the delicious scent was coming from." Charley said. "Oh, honey, I guess I've ignored you all day. I'm sorry. Here, folks, fresh pizza bites! Two for a dollar!"

Well, I was lucky to snort down my two pizza bites. It seems every little piggy in town wanted them too. The tray was gone in three minutes flat. It was enough for me to think I was really hungry. I needed a real nice quiet meal and I wanted one alone.

[8]

WE NOW HAD TWO AND half weeks before the Prickleberry Pie Contest took place. It seemed everyone was interested. The town was showing a lot of enthusiasm. A decision had been made at the town meeting that the tasting and judging would actually take place at the Chuckwagon Café. Lou and Kathy Evans felt that it would be the most logical place to accommodate all the entries. Tag Morton, at the weekly town meeting thought that security should be an issue. We need to keep the judges in the Café while the townfolk stays outside. Great, I thought. It will be like watching animals at the zoo. We'll be able to watch them through the glass window. Kathy said that they could cordon off a portion of the Café. Nobody wanted them to harass the judges. Charley said it would probably be a good idea. We didn't want anyone to pressure the judges on what selection to give a blue ribbon.

Several women had come into the store during the last few days selecting several special ingredients. I believed them to be some of the competition we'd see at the contest. Lucky for me that I had had Dale Woods build me a special fruit bin and presentation table. Right now that bin stood outside the shop laden with the freshest summer fruit anyone could offer. The cling and freestone peaches were the best I have tasted in years. I purchased several Ben Davis and King Solomon apples from the Edwards' orchard for sale. These heirloom summer apples were so tasty, I just had to bake an old fashioned pie myself. The Edwards family were surprised that I resold them in our shop when I told them.

"We thought we did a right smart business on our own, but Missy you sure proved us wrong. We're mighty obliged to ya, that's for shor, for sellin' our apples any aways."

"Well, Mr. Edwards, Charley and I are in the business to promote local produce. You sell the best apples around. I feel privileged when I can purchase some crates of them and offer them up for sale. I hope you know, we don't put that much of a markup on them. Just enough to keep the customers coming in the door," I told Mr. Edwards when he delivered another four crates.

All morning long I heard hammering and sawing from next door at the Antique Stop. It was starting to grate on my nerves. Ever since I discovered I had fallen into the aging process of menopause, I had been a little testy. Charley had ignored my little snap-backs. I know I need to watch myself and prevent me from really riding my broom sometimes.

Yes, even the Antique Stop was gilding the lily. Well, in my mind, they needed a little sprucing up. The owners, Alan and Meg Patton, in my mind, never really cared about how their shop looked inside or outside. Now, due to the pie contest, it had become a priority. They never came to the weekly town meetings either but they seemed to touch base with other citizens. The Pattons have always been a little eccentric. It would be interesting to see how they improve their shop and whether they get involved in the local activities. I would expect that they know their business will pick up. One can't just wait a few hours while pies are being judged without doing something. Plenty of people will browse in the Antique Stop to kill time.

I realized Charley had been in the back room making several phone calls while I had been preparing the lunch salads. Another sheet of cookies were ready to be pulled from the oven and he got up out of his chair and pulled them out automatically like some sort of robot. Then I saw he was still talking on the phone with the line stretched out to the limit.

"Good news, Francine! I just got off the phone with Paul Child. James Beard and Julia have started their road trip. Jim was pretty excited. He purchased a new Cadillac, a white convertible, after the latest edition of Beard on Bread came off the press. He and Julia are traveling together. Paul thinks he is doing some sort of research. Oh crikey, I wonder if it's on pies. Wouldn't that be a trip? Hah!" Charley laughed. "To think he's traveling the countryside with Julia Child looking for local pie recipes! Oh, that's hilarious! Anyway, we can't reach either one of them now until they get here."

"That is good news. At least we know they are on their way. That sure will be a sight for sore eyes. James Beard driving a big gleaming white Cadillac convertible with Julia Child sitting in the front seat. My, I can just picture her sitting there with a scarf tied on her head, the ends snapping in the breeze. They will pull into town in style. Everyone will be amazed. Charley… maybe we should have had them come in by limousine instead. You know, a bigger celebrity showpiece. What do you think?" I asked.

"I already went down that road with Jim. He told me that they were driving.

He wants to come into town on his own power. Oh, and guess what else?" "I am sure I couldn't guess, Charley, what?" I quizzed.

"Minnie Pearl is bringing Roy Clarke with her. Yeah, Roy Clarke. Isn't that great?" Charley grinned. "Hee Haw is on hiatus. Buck Owens is doin' some pickin' and grinnin' on his own. He's doing some country fairs and such.

Minnie asked Roy to come with her."

"That IS great news. I love Roy Clarke. He always reminded me of Uncle Roger." Now I was getting excited.

"I was thinking, Francine, that Roy can entertain the troops. While Jim, Julia, Irma and Minnie are in the Café judging the pies, Roy can play his banjo. Oh, this will be fun. This is better than I hoped for." Charley stepped forward and gave me a peck on the forehead. "I love you," he boomed.

Charley then turned and stepped out from the counter and walked out the door. I saw him gesture to Lou Evans and step towards the corner of the building facing the highway. From the window, I saw Whitey standing there too, smoking a cigarette. My distraction turned to the customers standing at the counter waiting for checking out their groceries and two construction guys were waiting on me finishing their sandwiches. Once I glanced out again and saw the three of them standing there eating cherries from my fruit bin, spitting pits into the highway, I was ready to go out and yell at Charley for eating up my profits when Pamela walked in.

"Dear, would you have any fresh figs today? I am so dying for some nice little tartlets" she asked.

"No, sorry, Pamela, but I do have a couple jars of Montgomery's Finest fig preserves. They make nice little tarts or cookies. The perfect little Southern treat for a summer tea time, don't you think?" I asked.

"Yes, I'll take two jars and one of those lemon pepper rotisserie chickens," She answered. "Francine, with all this hubbub going on, if you need some help in the store, please call me. I would love it if I could give you some assistance."

"If the opportunity comes up, I'll be sure to call you. That will be seven dollars and thirty-eight cents." I reported.

For whatever reason, this woman sometimes really tried my patience. I can't explain it. I hope I was not rude to her. She just bugs me sometimes. Maybe I am just striking out at her because she always gets stuff out of me. Personal stuff that I never verbalize to any one. Maybe I'm just in one of my moods. This menopause shortness. I must try to be nice to her, I keep telling myself. She means well, but she justs…uh…uh…uh. Oh well.

"Thank you, Pamela. I really appreciate it. By the way, are you entering?" I queried.

"What? Am I entering? Entering what?" she asked.

"Oh never mind. I should not have asked. I was just curious though. Are you entering the pie contest? You don't have to answer. A lot of people don't like to say that. Some sort of superstition and the like." I backed off. Why did I start running off at the mouth with this?

"No dear. I haven't decided." She responded.

"Oh. Okay then, have a good day!" I said as I watched her walk out the door.

I turned my attention back to the store and thought since the store had been cleared of customers, I could take some time to do some restocking on the shelves. I grabbed a box of mixed jams and jellies, slit open the top and proceeded to walk out into the main store area. Charley was still outside. Charley, still outside! Oh, anger started to rush forward. I need to tell him to come in and help me with this. I need some help from him in the store today. I will be so glad when this pie contest business is over. I stood up and saw something from the corner of my eye. My head turned and saw Pamela Wimbledon marching back in. Oh God, give me strength!

"Dear,…dear… come with me!" She said authoritatively and grabbed my arm.

She pulled me out the door and turned left to the front corner of the store. The same corner where Charley, Lou and Whitey had been chewing the fat for too long. I suddenly saw Charley sitting and leaning against the building. His head was down. Whitey had turned away from him looking down the highway. Lou was bent down beside him. I knelt down beside them. Lou put his arm around my shoulder.

"Honey, he's gone. We've called for the ambulance but it's too late. We couldn't save him." Lou's voice cracked.

I could hear Whitey sobbing, his shoulders heaving up and down. In the distance, I heard an emergency siren and I looked at Charley and knew it was true. Charley was not breathing and was completely grey. My body sank down to his and I grabbed his shirt. "Charley!" I screamed with only that deep bottom of the soul desperation real fear can provide. I continued to shake him and yell. "Charley! Charley! Oh my God! Charley! Please! Please!" I saw fingers try to pry mine off Charley's shirt and a voice asking me to let him go. My eyes, blurred with tears, still staring into Charley's face. Please, just give me a flicker of life from those eyes. Please God! I felt someone try to pull me up and again telling me to let him go. I was unable to move.

"I love you, old man" I told him as I ran my fingers down his cheek. "I love you!" I held onto his arm, already lifeless. I wanted to shake him, yell at him "Come back, come back, don't leave me here!" But I couldn't. I was stunned. I fell into a deep shock. I was frozen.

The paramedics had arrived. I kissed Charley this one last time lightly on his head as Lou helped me to my feet. They felt for a pulse, looked for any sign of respiration, and gave each other an unspoken signal to load him onto the gurney and cover him up. I stood watching as they loaded him into the ambulance and closed the doors. Lou held onto me and then walked me away from the curbside. I heard Whitey tell the paramedics, "Simpson, Simpson… Charley." Vaguely, I heard some conversation, but nothing to me was important. Nothing made sense. I was swirling in a blur of unreality.

"I'm so sorry, hon. Soooo… sorry. We'll do everything we can to help you." Lou whispered. "I'll get the information where they are taking him. We'll make arrangements to go down there later."

"Come dear," Pamela said, "come back in, we'll have a nice cup o' tea while we wait". She held my other arm leading me back into the store. Lou turned and latched the lock.

The rest of the afternoon was primarily a fog. I remember sitting in the store's back room with Pamela and Lou. Then Lou took me home. Pamela, obviously, had her chance to run the store. She promised to take over this afternoon and reopen for business today and tomorrow. At this point, I could care less. I've lost my husband, the love of my life. I can't think. I don't know where to start or begin.

[9]

IN THE MORNING, I FOUND myself sitting in a lounge chair on the back patio in my bathrobe drinking coffee. My mind was still a blank but obviously I had done some things automatically, like take a shower, make a pot of coffee. What else had I done? I heard the side gate slam shut.

"Hello? Francine? Honey, it's me and Kathy, are you OK?" Lou asked. "Listen, we rang the bell and we didn't get an answer. I hope you don't mind.

How are you holding up?"

I sat there. I looked up. I could see tears welling up in Kathy's eyes. Lou's were bloodshot. I could only imagine how bad mine were. I probably looked like some mad Frenchwoman from an old historical movie with bad makeup. Oh God, am I sitting here with my robe open? I shifted my robe tighter around me.

"Look, we know you need some time alone. You also need some time to make arrangements. If there is anything we can do, we will. Let me tell you a few things. First, Pamela opened your shop this morning and she's doing great. She has her niece with her and we are sure that they will run your place just fine. She's baked bread, pastries, cookies and lots of stuff this morning already. The store is stocked up on all the shelves, she's cleaned everything and she gave me your money bag last night. I gave her some cash to open with this morning. If you want, I'll bank it for you today." I nodded and weakly smiled.

"Pamela will continue as long as you need her. Now, second. Charley told me a lot of what his plans were for this Prickleberry Pie Contest. I will be the Master of Ceremonies and handle everything that Charley would have. I may need your help with some things, but we'll cross that bridge later. No worries, OK? I may need his day planner to cover some things. I think it's in the store. With your permission, I'll take it and work from it. Is that alright with you?" I nodded again.

"Thirdly, last night was our weekly meeting. I put a sign on your door and moved the meeting to our café. I let the town know what happened yesterday. That we lost a great man. Now, I can't tell you what to do, but seeing as how that Charley may not have been a real religious man, I don't know about how you feel about having a funeral. I know this is a very personal thing. With everything goin' on an' all, and don't get me wrong, having a funeral right now is kinda bad timing. We were thinkin' that maybe…"

"Lou," I answered, "it is kinda a personal thing. I don't think that Charley ever would want a funeral, you know? My plan is that I go to the mortuary today and arrange for his remains. What happens to him is my business. But… and I think it is fitting for him. We have a community memorial service for him and that it be held after this pie contest thing. I can't think it wise to put a damper on something that he so wanted to have. The purpose of this whole thing was to help Silent Springs."

"That would be real nice, honey." Kathy said as she wiped an eye. "We'll leave you alone now with your thoughts. Come on, Lou." She gave me a hug and tugged on his shirt.

I have no idea how long I sat there vegged out. It could have been an hour, it could have been a day or two. I can't really remember. I do remember my anger. Charley, how could you have done this to me? How could you have left me like this? How could you leave me and make me handle all this pie contest stuff? You know I'm not that good with it. All the planning, the arrangements, all the people. You know I'm shy. I have fear. Real fear. Fear of being alone. Oh Charley. Why?

I broke into another crying jag. One of those hysterical hiccupping sessions like a four year old. I just couldn't stop.

When I came back to reality hours later, I was in bed, hugging and smelling his pillow. His scent was still on the pillow. I remembered his last words to me, "I love you". Those three words gave me the strength. I have a life, a home, a business, a community, a pie contest, friends that care, faith. I dried my tears. I have to move on. Yet, deep down, I can't believe that he is gone. I have a sense he is with me but not here. Charley, where are you? My head is pounding and ready to split. Charley…

[10]

I LEFT THE HOUSE FOR the shop in the morning, on such a clear bright day, looking forward to a cup of fresh brewed espresso. The sun already hot shining in a cerulean sky, my favorite, giving me the strength to literally move forward. Yes, I knew I'd have to play the widow deck cards for a while, which I really didn't want to do, didn't want to play the martyr, didn't want to publicly show my grief, there's a lot of baggage I'd have to deal with for a while. Just make the best of it and work it through. Suddenly, my mind filled with another time. A long time ago. A time when I was a little girl and lost my beloved kitty cat, Miss Fluff. Words came flowing back from my dad when he saw how heartbroken I was. "We have to be a brave soldier," he told me, Then he gave me a hug and left me alone to grieve silently.

Oh my gosh! I arrived at the store and found that Pamela had made some changes. It was beautiful, gorgeous. She had added some decorating touches, arranged things differently, baked everything for the day, and was working on the salads and other nibbles. The shelves were all neat, clean, well-stocked. I noticed that she had taken it upon herself to order additional merchandise which was on the shelf and looked wonderful. The new products were class-A. It was terrific.

"Pamela, this is amazing! It's wonderful! You're too good to me!" I said and I meant it. I walked over to her and gave her a hug. "You're either my fairy godmother or my guardian angel!"

"Either one, I suppose. All in a day's work! Whatever flies your kite. How are you, dear? You know how we English are. Buck up, pip-pip, be a good soldier now. I took the liberty of making a few changes while you were out. I hope you approve."

"Oh, I do! I do! Hey, we need to talk. I owe you so much for everything you've done. You probably want to stop now that I'm back." Strange, she brought up the soldier thing too, I thought.

"Not at all. I am here for the long-haul. I don't ask for much Miss, just keep me on and I'll be your best partner." She said, whisking a bowl of pistachio pudding.

"Oh, hold your horses! Looks like Lucky's making an appearance. Of all things…" Pamela sighed.

I heard her expel deep breath, then suck in more air and held it.

I glanced out the window and saw a blond head bounce towards the door. Ugh! It was Lucky, that strange little lady that speaks in riddles and nursery rhymes. I didn't have much patience for her and apparently Pamela didn't either.

"Sugar for my tea,

Sugar for my tart,

Anything sweet, for my lovely sweetheart!

Would you still have any pearl sugar to put in my cart?"

"Yes, I do, Mam." I answered as I walked over to the shelf with the imported Swedish pearl sugar and large sugar granules that looked like the big salt on pretzels. Would you care for anything else?"

Lucky shook her head answering in a negative manner. I rang her up and bagged her boxed sugar in my signature special bag. She left silently wherein Pamela and I exploded into crying laughter. The tears were streaming down our faces.

"I needed that. That felt pretty good." My face hurt as I smiled at Pamela. We both looked at each other and burst again into uncontrolled laughter.

During the next few days, Pamela and I worked into a routine and things were going smoothly. It was as if Charley was still here. Pamela turned out to be quite the baker. In fact, our daily sales had actually increased. I really can't attribute it to anything. Sometimes I think that maybe people feel sorry for me and decide that they should come in and buy something to keep the widow going. But it really doesn't appear to be the case. Pamela has baked and offered a better and larger selection of goods than we offered before. We've brought in a few new items and offered more.

We had a week and a half to go before Pie Contest Day. The Antique Stop had finished their renovation. The building was now stunning. They set up several large pots of plants in front of their store. When Pamela saw them, she did the same thing, only bigger, more colorful and beautiful. She had planted herbs with the flowers and the fragrance that exuded from them was sheer intoxicating. On the corner of the store where Charley had collapsed, Pamela had placed a humongous pot with an Italian cypress in it with creeping purple phlox curled over the edge. How she ever moved it into place, I will never know. Somehow she knew. She knew every time I stood outside and relived my terrible nightmare looking at that spot. Now the Italian cypress stood guard to keep me from thinking about it. What she didn't know was that it stood as a replacement for Charley. I kept thinking the tree was him standing there protecting the store.

When Pamela added some stylish curtains to our windows, the Antique Stop did some window dressing. It seems quite a rivalry has sprung up.

The morning for a Wednesday was tremendously busy. I couldn't recall a Wednesday quite this heavy ever. I told Pamela that if this keeps up, we'd have to hire us a helper. While "I was fixing an order for three "fisherman special – packed lunch", a tall young man came in and stood at the counter.

"Be with you in just a minute," I said.

"Where's Charley? I need Charley!" The tall man barked.

Everyone in the store turned around and stared. Pamela dropped a box of cookies that she had been packing on the counter and bounded up to the young man. "We'll have none o' that, here!" She said as she poked him in the chest.

"I'm looking for Charley, where is he?" Again the man bellowed in a demanding voice.

"I'm Francine Simson, Charley's wife. Can I help you?

"No, I want Charley! Get him for me immediately!"

"I'm sorry, but that's impossible." I answered very calmly. I put my index finger to my mouth signaling to him to be silent. "Charley passed away last week. He can't…be here. Now what is it that I can help you with?" I quietly let out a sigh. How I wish Charley was here too. I waited for the man to compute.

"Oh. Sorry, Mam… I didn't know." He sputtered.

"That's obvious, son. Now, tell Mrs. Simson what you need." Pamela interjected.

"My name is Tim Clary. I work for Peregrine Publishing. Charley signed a contract for a cookbook. He completed the preface and other portions of the book but he was supposed to get me the rest of it. We need to publish the book immediately because it is supposed to be ready to sell at the Prickleberry Pie Contest as a fundraiser. I need it now. We're running out of time."

"I see." I said. "What parts are you missing?"

"Well, most of it. We need the recipes that are entered in the contest as well as the biographies of the bakers who presented their wares for judging at the contest."

Well, this was a mind-blower. No wonder Charley had a blow out. He had so much going on it was doubtful Superman could have kept up.

"Mr. Clary," I answered. "I will try to get you that information as quickly as I can. Please leave me your card. I will contact you as soon as I have the draft ready. How much time do we have? What I mean is, what is your absolute dropdead date? Pardon the pun, if you will."

"I honestly don't know. I'll have to check with my boss. He was the one that sent me over here. Anyway, I think if we have everything by Thursday, we should publish and bind it on Friday for delivery on Saturday morning. I think that's the best we can do. We really need it sooner to do this. And Mrs. Simson? The money is non-refundable. We have to publish it, we can't give Mr. Simson's money back in any case. We've already printed the covers, certain pages, photos, the ads. In other words, we've already sunk money into this as well."

"I understand, Mr. Clary. Thank you. I will be in touch with you. Pamela, I'm going over to see Lou Evans. Can you hold down the fort for a few minutes?" Excuse me, Mr. Clary, I must go. Oh, and Pamela, would you call Ruta Mae Elkins and ask her to come over at 2 PM today? I have a project for her. Thanks!"

I walked out of the grocery and headed across the town square. It was time that Lou and Kathy knew I was back.

Lou had given me the key to the entry box in the town square and I retrieved twenty-four entries. I locked the box and took the key back to Lou.

"Did you know that he contracted a cookbook for this thing?" I asked.

"Sure, we all do. All the merchants here on the square paid for advertising in it. I think it is best advertising we've had in years!" Lou answered.

"I think it's been your only advertising." I smiled.

"Yeah," Lou responded. "Wish I had thought about it. That man, he surprised me every day. His mind was just a whorl of wheels."

"Well, I gotta go, Lou. I've got a lot more to do now than I thought I had when I first woke up this morning." I turned and started walking out of the Chuckwagon. "Lou?" I said quietly, "Thanks. Thanks to you and Kathy. Your help and support really mean a lot to me." My eyes started to tear up and I knew I had to make a quick exit.

In the office, I found another stack of entries. Now we had a total of one hundred and one. If every contestant baked just one pie, we'd have over a hundred. Wonder if they made more? Oh my, this is crazy. Now my mind starting turning like a whorl of wheels, in Lou's terminology. How many pies could we expect? Was there any way to gauge them? Was there a limit? Do the judges need two pies per entry? One for taste and one for appearance? Oh, this was just getting too much for me to think about. It was exponentially expanding.

Ruta Mae bounced into the grocery at two o'clock with her steno pad and pen. She had a big smile on her face and she seemed sincerely excited. I wondered if I expected too much from her. I hope she can meet the guidelines. The worst part was the pressure the publisher had put me on. Between Ruta Mae and myself, we'd have to hustle. I put a plan of action together and relayed it to her as best I could. The incentive for Ruta Mae would be that she would be listed as an author. This would be quite a feat and a feather tucked into her

THE PRICKLEBERRY PIE CONTEST

cap. She could finally be known as an author, a journalist, anything she wanted to spin, if we could just complete this. I photocopied all the entries and gave Ruta Mae a folder full of copies. She left the store so excitedly, she literally flew out the door.

"See you tomorrow! Good luck!" I yelled as she left.

I joined Pamela at the counter and went back to work. Mark Patterson, the county sheriff stopped in for a couple of cookies.

"I had to come back in and buy me a coupla' more of these." He pointed to what Pamela had been calling 'raspberry crowns'.

I knew that Mark always ate a sausage biscuit at the café with a coffee in the morning and then stopped in for a few cookies that he called "for the road". But lately, Pamela's wares were more enticing than Charley's ever were. I put three in a small bag and charged him seventy-five cents.

"Francine, these are just the best. No offense, but your cookies are much better now that you ladies are making them. I mean, Charley made good cookies but they all were heavy, filled with fruit and nuts, and chocolate chips, butterscotch pieces and whatnot, but these, these are awesome!"

"Why, thanks, Mark! Actually, I was just thinking the same thing. God knows Charley was a great chef, but that is different than being a baker. You're right. Charley's stuff was more, manly, hearty. Now don't get offended by that! I think that Pamela and I are baking crisp, fragile delights than what Charley could do."

"You're absolutely right about that. Hey, want to let you know that we've stepped up our patrol in town. We're goin' ta get a lot of traffic and outsiders. This town has never seen so many strangers or will anyway. Charley had tole me that he wasn't so concerned about people gettin' ripped, but he was sure worried about the celebrity's safety. Jus' so you know." Mark admitted. "Ma wife won't be too happy if I gain some more weight, ah'm jus' bustin' outta my uniform but this place is jus' too hard to resist right now." With that, he picked up a saran-wrapped shortbread cookie and plunked down another quarter.

When the sheriff semi-waddled out the door, I turned and washed my hands. I told Pamela that I was going to be in the backroom for a while. I returned to my work station and picked up the entries. I had given Ruta Mae copies but really I had never looked at them. Now, I had the chance. My curiosity had piqued. Who has entered and what are they making?

"Fields of daisies and a picnic spread!" Barked right out of my mouth. I startled myself. My back did a body slam into the chair causing it to screech backwards across the floor. I held my hand to my chest where my heart pounded and sucked in a breath.

"Francine, dear, are you alright?" Pamela yelled back.

"Why yes…uh…don't worry, I'm OK," I answered. I didn't want her snooping around with this as well.

I looked at the entries and my mind buzzed. How many categories are there? Let's see, I saw apple, cherry, fruit, custard, cream, nut, sweetie, savory. Savory? What's savory? Hey, wait. What's sweetie? I had to call Lou. Someplace Charley kept a master list of pie categories, where is it? I looked around his desk, folders he kept and I could not find anything that resembled a list. Ohmigosh! For each category, there must a prize and a prize for best of show. What are we giving, ribbons? Oh-my-gosh, again! I never even thought about all this until now. What was I thinking? Pie is pie, I guess. Who knew it could be so complicated?

While I was occupied looking at the entries, Pamela continued in the front of the store handling customers as usual. I heard the occasional banter with customers but didn't pay much attention. I have to admit that Pamela is really a godsend to me. She's helped tremendously. Not only as a new best friend, she's become a mother substitute. I really could not have made it through the last couple of weeks without her. Coming back to reality, I moved to the counter to help her. She was engaged with a young man I think I've seen before. She helped him pick out a couple of cookies. He then asked a remarkable question. Anyway, I thought so at the time. I was thinking he was so thoughtful.

"I have an acquaintance who's been very ill. " He said. "Is there anything here that could help? I mean, if someone's been sick, is there anything that's really good for them?"

"Well, son," Pamela said, "I assume you are asking if it's healthy? Or would something hurt a sick person unintentionally, is that what you're worried about? Some people feel better with food they know, it's called comfort food. What your mama fed you when you were little. Like mac and cheese. Or something you like. No one could resist a chocolate chip cookie unless you were allergic to chocolate. An oatmeal raisin cookie could help someone. The fiber in the oatmeal and has a higher amount of protein to beef you back up. I guess it all depends."

"That's my dilemma, mam. I don't know what would work in this instance." He said sincerely.

"All right, you say this friend has been ill. My family has been prone to drinking hot tea when we feel puny. I'd recommend something simple like these lovely shortbreads. They go well with a 'cuppa'. I'd recommend you take a half dozen. Serve it with a nice cup of tea. It should perk your friend right up. Let me know how it works."

"Thanks, Mam. Sounds like a plan. I'll let you know, for sure."

"You do that, son. That'll be $2.20. Oh, do you need tea? Should I add that on?"

"No, Mam, I'm good. Here's two and a quarter. Keep the change. Thanks for your advice." The young man turned with our signature bag of shortbread and started out the door. Then quietly, he said "I think there's been a terrible mistake."

"Pardon?" Pamela inquired.

The young man just shook his head and left.

Why did I have an uneasy feeling watching that young man exit the store? I couldn't tell Pamela that the local mortuary couldn't find Charley at the County Coroner's Office. Nor did the Coroner's Office know anything about my Charley. The ambulance didn't have information on where they had taken Charley. The last telephone conversation I had with them suggested that the County takes their time in processing the paper work. They would inform me when it was ready. I couldn't talk to Pamela about this. Kathy and Lou had no knowledge either. I would just have to deal with this when all the hullabaloo was over.

[11]

WEDNESDAY MORNING. SURPRISINGLY, THE DAY started overcast. It was warm with a cool breeze. It felt tropical outside. Well, let it rain. We need a good soaking in the town square and then a day or two to dry up to make it really beautiful. Pamela and I started early baking breads. Because of the moisture in the air, the bread dough was acting a little testy today. I hope it wasn't going to rub off onto one of my mood swings. I had a lot of ground to cover. Balmy is the last thing I need to feel mentally, but climatologically would be acceptable.

The fresh fruit delivery this morning was unbelievable. Pamela and I decided to make a little precursor to pies. We prepared little fruit tarts. I baked crispy little tart cups while Pamela washed beautiful little strawberries, currants, blueberries, raspberries and peaches. We made a little custard and topped it in the baked cups with the fruit. Pamela heated up currant jelly and apricot jam and slowly poured them over the tarts, depending on the variety of fruit. They sparkled like jewels. Our display cases were gorgeous. No one would be able to walk away without purchasing something, they beckoned, they called "eat me!".

"Oh dear, here she comes again!" I told Pamela. "Lucky's back." I watched Lucky walk from the square across the street straight towards our door.

"Oh Lord, give me patience." I heard Pamela say.

Lucky walked in and headed straight for the counter.

"Peter Piper picked a peck of pickled peppers,

How many pecks of pickled peppers did Peter Piper pick?"

"You'll have to ask him when he gets back." I answered.

THE PRICKLEBERRY PIE CONTEST

"Good one!" Lucky mumbled and giggled slightly. "Prickleberry Pie, Prickleberry Pee, your box is out of entries, give one to me!"

"Oh, you need an entry form? Hold on a minute." I walked to the backroom and brought out a blank. "I didn't realize the box was empty. Thanks for letting me know."

Lucky grabbed her entry form and silently left the shop.

"Francine, you are terrible! I would never believe that you would give her a smart-ass answer like that." Pamela responded with a smile on her face. "That was really funny."

"And Pamela, I would never believe that you would say the word "smart-ass! Did you hear her say "Good one!" to me? "

"No, I didn't hear her say that."

"Yes, she did. And, she giggled after she said it. I think she enjoyed it. I think this is a big put-on."

"Oh, Francine, what did she mean by Prickleberry Pee? Do you think she will really enter the contest? Will she pee in her pie? Does Pee stand for poison? I think I am getting very concerned. Oh, what do you think we should do? Francine?" Pamela seemed worried.

"She's getting to you. You are responding just the way she wants you to. Oh Pamela, you are so funny!" I started laughing. "Lucky, ooooohh, Lucky, oooooh, Lucky. BOO!"

She looked at me and shook her head. Maybe we are both losing our minds. At least I can make an excuse. I better make an effort and put some replacement entries in the box, just in case.

Lou called at half past ten and reported that he had just picked up all the prizes, ribbons, trophies and certificates. What a relief that was. Maybe I can focus on just working today. Deep in my mind, however, I kept thinking about Ruta Mae and what progress she was making. I felt guilty about pulling her away from her parents business. But I had my own to think about. Also, this was the best opportunity that girl has had in starting a dream of her own. I know I was really asking too much of her and I feel bad about it, still, let's see what she's made of…

Friday 1:30 AM is what my alarm clock is blinking in my face. I literally had passed out from fatigue earlier. Now I woke up and can't get back to sleep. Everything is swirling around my head. The judges are coming tomorrow, the pie contest will begin. What's left to do? Oh Charley, I wish you were here. I miss you, honey. The cookbook is going into print today. The cookbook! Oh my, that's right. Ruta Mae had dropped off a copy of the manuscript before she took the original to the printers at ten P.M. I hope she got it there in time. I need to take a look at how she did. I reached down to my nightstand where I had left it before I had fallen asleep and opened to the first page.

APPLES

Tom and Dottie Mays own an apple orchard near the Prickleberry Pie Contest. The Mays live in a well-groomed white farmhouse with a large frog pond out front. The house is surrounded by a crescent of thin woods and then the rest of their acreage is covered in apple trees. I met with Dottie in her kitchen while she baked her entries for the competition.

"You see this here kitchen?" She asked as she pointed her wooden spoon and spun 360 degrees around. "This kitchen is the whole original log cabin built in the 1840s. There is quite a family story about this house and our apple orchard.

Would you like to hear me tell it?" She asked.

"Yes, Mam, I would," I answered.

"As you know, I was born in this here house. I've lived here all my life, ALL my life. I was born in 1927 right here. As the story goes, my Daddy hired on at my Grandpap's farm and fell in love with his only daughter. At that time, Grandpap only had one child, his daughter, my momma. There were no sons to help him with the farm. My Daddy was an orphan. He had nothing to offer her, but he worked hard and he was smart. My Daddy married my Momma and they lived with my grandparents for nearly three years. As the new century was approaching, he told my momma that the new year would bring them prosperity. He was an enterprising young man. He didn't earn much from Grandpap, but he did save. He did many things to earn money and one day, he told my momma that he was goin' to the woods and find him some honey trees. He would bring home honey comb and process them. He wanted to sell jars of honey at the local farmers' market. He left home early one fall morning where it drizzled and misted and was so foggy in places he couldn't hardly see his hand in front of his face. He walked for nearly three hours in the woods looking for an old honey tree he remembered seeing. Across one shoulder was a huge canvas bag he had sewn years earlier as a boy. He carried a saw, some hand tools, several jars, a canteen of fresh spring water and a sausage biscuit.

In the meantime, Daddy left Momma at home tending to her mother. Grandmama had taken ill and had been bed-ridden for nearly three weeks. Grandmama could not keep any food down. Everyone was afraid that she had the consumption. She was pale and weak, but otherwise was in no pain. Momma, who was expecting her first child, acted as her nurse and housekeeper. She was fatigued and very tired. Daddy thought that the taste of honey would greatly improve her condition and give her much needed energy.

Daddy found that as he walked in the woods, the forest floor was covered with a foot of fallen leaves. Everything was a brown color and with the mist, it was difficult to see. Suddenly, he tripped over something and as he corrected himself, he looked back. There was an old grizzled man barely alive, sitting propped up next to a tree with his legs extended out. He was wearing buckskins.

"Sir! Sir! Are you alive?" My Daddy asked him.

The old man grunted, and then said "Yeah, ah am, the Lord hasn't seen fit to take me home yet, but I feel I'm a goner." He whispered.

My Daddy had discovered that the man had been bitten by a timber rattler. He looked to be an old leatherwood. The type of man that once lived here in the woods back in the old days. My Daddy looked at the bite and saw that it was bad. He cleaned the wound as best he could and then told the man that he was taking him back to town. Daddy told him that he could not leave a man to die in the woods alone. The man admitted that he had not eaten in days. He was very weak. Daddy gave him his sausage biscuit and the spring water he had in a canteen. Then he placed his canvas satchel in the crook of a tree and hefted the man across his shoulder.

"Fella, please, take my bag and leave me be!" the old man cried. Daddy would not hear of it. "Ok, then fella, take my bag. If anything happens, keep my bag," He pleaded.

Daddy carried him for hours, down through the hollows, across the knobs, and finally reached town. All through the day, Daddy spoke to him. Told him about his life, his dreams. The man said he knew of him. Said he had been told that Daddy was a good man, knew his skills, his ambition. Then he made a surprising statement. He told Daddy that he had watched him, followed him and said that in his heart, he would find him again. That was such an odd statement, Daddy thought. He admitted to Daddy that he had done wrong in his life and he truly regretted the bad things. Said it might be too late to make it good. He was worried the Lord wouldn't accept him into heaven. The man grew silent and while Daddy listened, he kept walking, suddenly finding himself at Dr. Hopkin's house. He told the doctor of how he had found him in the woods. The doctor and his wife kept a room for patients that occasionally found their way to need medical help. In 1900, there was no hospital here. People were treated at home. In the event of travelers coming through the area, Dr. Hopkins was the only doctor available for a days' ride.

Daddy helped Doctor Hopkins and his wife clean up the old man and put him to bed. Then he assisted the doctor again with the wound and left him for the night. Daddy told the doctor that the old man was concerned about the leather bag he had Daddy carry for him. He asked Doctor and Mrs. Hopkins to hold it for safe keeping.

Daddy returned the Grandpap's farm and told everyone about finding the old man propped up against a tree. He told Grandpap that on his next free day, he would again try to find his canvas satchel and the honey tree. He apologized to Momma for not bringing home any honey. Another set back in their plans to buy their own home.

Business returned as usual to the farm. The men farmed and Momma nursed her mother who was still bed-ridden. A few days later, at dinner time, Dr. Hopkins arrived. He was offered dinner and he refused it saying that he and the missus had eaten earlier. He was

THE PRICKLEBERRY PIE CONTEST

here to relay some important information. He reported that the old man had passed on. Daddy half expected it since the old man had been in bad shape. The doctor said that the old man had asked him to write a will which he was obliged to do. The man had given him specific instructions and those he was following up with now. Doctor Hopkins pulled an envelope out of his jacket which he opened and read. It was the last will and testament of the old man. Surprisingly, the old man left all his worldly possessions to my Daddy. In addition, the doctor was told to give the leather bag to Daddy where he would find his inheritance. When they opened the leather bag, they found an old map indicating some property, papers relating to the property and five gold pieces.

After checking with an attorney and filing property ownership, paying property taxes, Daddy and Grandpap then went in search for the property. That is this same property I live on. Back then, they only found the log cabin and it was in good condition. The property was mostly deep woods then. There was a nice fresh spring, which is now our frog pond. Back then there was a small stream that ran from the pond area and moved across to the south.

Daddy, being an honorable man, told Grandpap that he and Momma would move after the crops were planted in the spring. This would give Grandpap time to find a new man. But also, that Daddy could do the hard work needed and make sure the crops were planted well and started. Momma was concerned because Grandmama was still ill and she didn't want to leave her. When Spring arrived, one day Daddy was plowing a field. Grandpap was working with the cattle and suddenly Grandmama started screaming. Momma ran to her and tried to help her. Momma noticed that Grandmama's stomach was tightening up and then relaxing. Suddenly, she realized all along with Grandmama's problem had been. She called out to Daddy and caught his eye. Sensing something was wrong he ran to the house. When she told him, he went to the field and jumped on the first horse and rode at lightning speed to Dr. Hopkins.

By now, Momma, being a new mother, realized that this was not going to be an easy birthing. My oldest brother, Lyle, seemed to sense that something was wrong and he started crying. Momma says he was only four months old at the time. Grandpap saw Daddy ride off and thought something was going on. He came into the house and simultaneously all three men arrived at the same time. That was the day Momma's twin brothers were born. As soon as they were born, Grandmama was fine. So, she wasn't going to die after all.

Momma and Daddy now knew that Grandpap's farm would be inherited by her baby brothers. It was now the time to move. They came to the log cabin and made a comfortable home. Daddy spent years clearing woods and growing crops. As the farmland and pastureland grew, so did the family. The cabin was woefully small as well as their savings. One night, a humongeous storm blew in. Momma thought the big red oak that was near the back of the cabin would fall through the roof. It seemed as though they were in the midst of a tornado. While the cabin walls held well, the roof flew off in pieces and the red oak lost several large limbs.

After the storm, my five older brothers helped Daddy cut down the red oak and replace the roof on the log cabin. It was then that Momma said it was time they enlarged the home. It was too small for seven people living in such a small room. While the boys cut limbs and stacked fire wood, Daddy spent time cutting down the large tree trunk. He stopped suddenly when he came to a knothole in the trunk. He called to Momma. When she came out of the cabin and they both peered into the knothole, they found a leather pouch lodged in the tree trunk. It seemed to take hours extricating the pouch. The tree had grown around the pouch and it was wedged tight in the interior wood. Once again, another miracle occurred. When they opened the pouch, they again found more gold pieces and this time, a note written on a piece of leather rolled up inside the pouch. The note said that the gold pieces belonged to "my son, Lonnie Upton. Please forgive me. I have loved you with all my heart, your father, Josiah. Most of my life I was known as Simon White."

On reading the note, Daddy staggered backwards and finally sat down on a log. Momma had tears in her eyes. Holding his shoulders, they cried together. My brothers were scared on seeing this. My parents were not the type of people that exhibited much emotion. My brothers could not understand what was happening. Daddy finally explained. "My real name is Lonnie Upton. I was always told that I was orphaned. I lived with several family members throughout my early years and then I was placed in an orphanage when the families could no longer afford to keep me. The man that left this money in this tree was my father. He is also the same man that left me this property. He was the man I found under the tree the day I went in search of the honey tree."

With the money they found in the tree that day, my parents were able to build this home" Dottie said.

"Wow, that's quite a story," this reporter said. "What I don't understand is how it relates to the apple orchard."

"Well, you are right on that account. I was born in 1927, right here in my own bedroom. I am the last of nine children. By then, my oldest brother was actually twenty-seven years old. I thought my parents were old by then, but I'm nearly their age now when I was born. I guess the women in my family tend to have change of life babies. Ha!

When the Great Depression hit, my parents were concerned as anyone in this country. Lucky for us, we had a farm, chickens, and cattle. But deep down, my Daddy was afraid that we'd lose all we owned. It wasn't that the bank owned the land, they didn't. We owned the property outright. But at the time, you had to pay the taxes. The County could take over your property if you weren't careful. As the depression continued, more people lost their property, their farms, their homes. There were droughts and plagues of insects. Many farmers lost their crops. After a while, even the Counties went bankrupt. No one could afford the taxes and no one could afford to buy the properties up for sale. My Daddy sat down and took stock of all we owned. Time to get rid of the most costly assets, he said. He sold off the cattle. He told Momma that it takes too much time and money to grow feed for cattle, too many cattle diseases to care for, too much time to run this portion of the farm. The boys were leaving home and he was doing most of the work by himself. One day he went away and left in the old red pickup truck and was gone for about a week. When he came home, he had a truckload of sticks.

Momma cried, "What have you done?" and he said it was going to be all right.

Daddy tilled the pasture and started planting apple trees. Everyone thought he was off his rocker. How could he afford planting trees? How could a man wait seven years to start harvesting crops worth while? Daddy had searched high and low for many varieties of apples. Ben Stars, King Solomon, all sorts of heirlooms. Because this area of the Ozarks has cedar trees, there is a tree disease called rust. This affects apple trees. So Daddy, after painstaking research and trial by error, learned which apple varieties were susceptible or not to rust. Throughout the years, the varieties continue to grow and vary. When WWII occurred, a lonely soldier arrived at our doorstep. Frail and thin recovering from war wounds, he asked for a job. Daddy saw the same look in his eyes that he recognized from his own. That would be my Tom. Tom came to work for us and we fell in love. It has been Tom's passion all these years to keep Daddy's orchard healthy and fruitful. He's planted Arkansas Blacks this year. We sure look forward to growing those. My parents are long gone now, but our apple orchard lives on.

Oh, it looks like the last two pies are ready. You see this inset in the wall where my oven is? That is the original fireplace from the log cabin. Yes, most people would say that my family has been lucky. I'd like to say I'll be lucky on Saturday when my pies win first place. In my family, we don't rely on luck. Our family's strength lies in faith, togetherness and an inherited desire to stay together and work hard. Most of all, we have a duty to grow the best healthiest apples anyone could ever eat.

Well, Miss, here's my pies for the contest and here's my treasured recipes."

"Thank you, Mrs. Mays, and good luck to you. Those ARE the best looking apple pies I've ever seen!"

THE PRICKLEBERRY PIE CONTEST

DOTTIE MAYS' OLD-FASHIONED APPLE PIE

6 large apples, any variety will do
1 cup sugar
¼ tsp. salt
1 tsp. ground cinnamon
2 T. all purpose flour
1 recipe Southern Pie Crust
1 T. butter

Preheat oven to 450 degrees. Peel, core, and slice apples. Place in a large mixing bowl. In a separate smaller bowl, mix together the sugar, salt, cinnamon and flour. When blended well, add the dry ingredients to the apples and stir in, being careful not to break the apple slices.

Line pie pan with half of the southern pie crust, then add apple mixture. Smooth apple mixture down so the filling is even throughout the pan. Dot top with butter then cover with the top crust. Crimp edge.

Bake in very hot over (450 degrees Fahrenheit) for 15 minutes, then reduce heat to moderate (350 degrees Fahrenheit) and bake for an additional 45 minutes.

Top crust should be a nice golden brown. Makes 1 9" pie.

Variations:

Peel, core and slice 1-2 large quince. Add to apples. Proceed as directed. The quince adds a delicate floral flavor to the pie. They may also provide a light pink or rosy color to the pie filling.
Add ½ cup fresh or dried blueberries to the apples.
Add ½ cup dried cherries to the apples.
Add ½ cup dried cranberries to the apples.

Substitute half the apples with peeled, cored and sliced pears. Reduce the cinnamon to ½ tsp.

Add 1 cup chopped fresh rhubarb to the apples. Increase flour to 2 Tablespoons, add ¼ tsp. nutmeg.

Add ½ cup fresh raspberries or fresh blackberries to the apples.

Substitute the sugar with honey to taste.

Brush milk lightly on the top crust and sprinkle with sugar.

GOLDEN APPLE PIE

6 large apples, can use golden delicious, antique yellow banana apple, Aurora or McIntosh apples
Juice from 1 lemon
1 cup sugar
1 tsp. lemon zest
½ tsp. cinnamon
¼ tsp. nutmeg
Pinch of mace
1 T. all purpose flour
½ cup golden raisins
½ cup chopped walnuts
1 recipe southern pie crust
Milk
1 T. sugar

Preheat oven to moderate 350 degrees Fahrenheit. Peel, core and slice apples, placing in large mixing bowl and add juice of 1 lemon. Stir well. This prevents the apples from darkening. In a separate bowl, mix together the sugar, lemon zest, spices and flour, then stir into the apples. Add the raisins and walnuts. Line a 9" pie pan with southern pie crust, add apple mixture, then cover top with crust. Crimp edge. Brush top with milk lightly, then sprinkle it with sugar.

Cut small slit in the center of the top. Bake for 1 hour until golden.

DUTCH APPLE PIE

6 large apples
1 cup sugar
Juice from 1 lemon
½ tsp. cinnamon
¼ tsp. nutmeg
1/2 recipe pate brisee
1 cup flour
1/3 cup white sugar
1/3 cup brown sugar, packed
¼ tsp cinnamon
¼ tsp nutmeg
1 stick unsalted butter
Pinch of salt
½ cup ground almonds

Preheat oven to 350 degrees Fahrenheit. Peel and core apples. Dice apples into 1 inch chunks. In large mixing bowl, stir the juice from 1 lemon into the apple dice. Add sugar and spices, mix well.

Lay pate brisee into 9" pie pan and flute edge in decorative manner.

In medium size bowl, add flour, sugars, spices, salt, ground almonds and stir.

Add butter, with your fingers, rub it into dry mixture until uniformly crumbly. Try not to overmix. This topping should look fluffy.

Pour apples into lined pie pan, smooth evenly for coverage. Sprinkle topping over apples, covering them to the edge. Bake for approximately 1 hour. Topping should be browned but not overly dark.

GAELIC ISLES APPLE PIE

For the shortbread crust, use your favorite shortbread recipe or:
1 egg, beaten
½ cup sugar
1 ½ cups flour
½ cup rice flour
Pinch of salt
1½ sticks unsalted butter, cut into small pieces

For Filling:
5-6 Golden Delicious Apples
¼ cup firmly packed light brown sugar
1 T. flour
½ tsp. cinnamon
Pinch of nutmeg

For crust, mix egg and sugar together in large mixer bowl. Using mixer, blend in the butter, until incorporated. Add flours and salt. Mixture should be crumbly. Take approximately 3/4s of the shortbread mixture and pat into bottom and sides of an 8 inch tart or cake pan. It is best to use a springform pan for this pie. Set aside the remainder ¼ of the shortbread crumbs. Keep shortbread pan and crumbs cool.

Heat oven to 400 degrees Fahrenheit.

Peel, core and slice apples. Place apples in large mixing bowl. Add light brown sugar, flour and spices, mixing well. Place in prepared pan, spreading to cover evenly. Sprinkle remaining shortbread crumbs on top.

Bake in oven for 15 minutes, then reduce heat to 350 degrees and continue baking for 25 minutes. Top should be light brown and apple filling is bubbly. Cool in pan at least a half hour before attempting to remove.

COUNTRY APPLE SNOW PIE

1 ½ cups crushed unsalted saltine crackers
6 T. unsalted butter, melted
1 envelope unflavored gelatin
½ cup water
½ cup sugar
Pinch of salt
¾ cup applesauce
¾ cup filtered apple juice or apple cider
Juice of 1 lemon
2 egg whites

Blend the crushed crackers and butter together and press into bottom and sides of a 9 inch pie pan. Reserve 1 tablespoon for topping. Chill for approximately 1 hour.

To make filling, add the ½ cup of water to a medium saucepan and sprinkle with the gelatin. Stir over low heat until gelatin dissolves, about 3 minutes. Stir in the sugar and salt, making sure they dissolve. Remove from heat. Add the applesauce, apple juice or cider and lemon juice, then chill the mixture for approximately 1 hour.

When mixture has thoroughly chilled, pour into a large mixing bowl, add the egg whites and whip at high speed for approximately 10 minutes. The mixture should be very light and fluffy. Pour into prepared crust. Chill, once again, for at least 3 hours. To serve, top with fresh sliced apples and sprinkle with reserved crumbs.

YE OLDE ENGLISH APPLE TOAD IN THE HOLE PIE

Custard:
3 large eggs
1/3 cup light brown sugar, packed
1 tsp. vanilla
1 ½ cups milk
¼ tsp nutmeg
½ tsp cinnamon
4 small apples
1 recipe pate brisee

Preheat oven to 350 degrees Fahrenheit. Line a 9 inch pie pan with pate brisee, finish edge decoratively.

Peel apples and cut in half, from top to bottom. Remove cores and place them face down in the pie pan. One apple half in the center and surrounded by the remainder.

Prepare custard by mixing the eggs, sugar, vanilla, milk and nutmeg together. Pour over the apples. Take pinches of the cinnamon and drop onto the apples to create "spots".

Bake for 40 minutes or until custard tests done.

COLONIAL INDIAN PUDDING APPLE PIE

1 standard pie crust
¾ cup light brown sugar, packed
½ cup whole wheat flour
¼ cup yellow cornmeal
½ tsp. cinnamon
½ tsp. allspice
4 T. unsalted butter, softened
1 ½ T. whipping cream

8 tart green apples, such as Granny Smith
1 tsp. flour
4 T. unsalted butter, softened
2 T. sugar
1/3 cup unsulphered molasses, sorghum, or dark corn syrup
1 tsp. cinnamon
½ tsp. allspice
¼ tsp. ground ginger

Preheat oven to 375 degrees Fahrenheit. Prepare topping by mixing together the brown sugar, whole wheat flour, cornmeal and spices. With your fingers, rub in the butter to form small pea size lumps, then add the whipping cream. Set aside. Peel, core and slice apples. In a large mixing bowl, toss apples with the flour. In a separate bowl, blend butter, sugar, molasses and spices until smooth, then pour over apples. Mound apples into prepared pie pan. Sprinkle topping over apples. Bake for 30 minutes, then reduce heat to 350 degrees Fahrenheit and continue baking for another 30 minutes.

AUTUMN APPLE PIE

½ cup raisins
½ cup smooth sippin' whiskey
8 large cooking apples
4 T. unsalted butter
1 cup sugar
2 T. quick cooking tapioca
1 tsp. cinnamon
¼ tsp. nutmeg
¼ tsp. ground ginger
Pinch of salt
½ cup chopped walnuts or pecans
2 tsp. apricot preserves, melted
1 T. milk

Sugar for sprinkling
1 recipe southern pie crust

Soak raisins in whiskey overnight.

Preheat oven to 450 degrees Fahrenheit. Peel, core and slice apples. In a medium mixing bowl, stir together the sugar, tapioca, spices, and salt. Set aside. In a large frying pan, melt butter and add the apples. Slowly stir apples and cook until soft, about 5 minutes. Turn off heat. To the apples, add the sugar/spice mixture, raisins and nuts. Stir together. Brush melted apricot preserves onto the prepared pie crust. Pour apple mixture on top.
For top crust, use leaf cookie cutter or prepare lattice strips. Form over apples in a decorative fashion. Brush with milk and sprinkle with sugar.
Bake at 450 degrees for 15 minutes, then reduce heat to 350 degrees Fahrenheit and continue baking for 30 minutes.

CARAMEL APPLE PIE

6 baking apples
¾ cup sugar
¼ cup light brown sugar
¼ cup orange juice
1 tsp. orange zest
1 recipe standard pie crust
½ cup chopped walnuts
1 T. cinnamon sugar
1 cup sugar
½ cup boiling water
2 T. heavy cream

Preheat oven to 350 degrees Fahrenheit. Peel, core and cut apples into half inch dice. Place them into large mixing bowl. Add both white and light brown sugar, orange juice and orange zest. Mix well. Place into prepared pie shell.

With top crust, cut and form into lattice crust over the apples. Sprinkle lattice with cinnamon sugar and chopped walnuts. Bake for 1 hour. Top should be golden brown. Remove from oven and allow pie to cool.

Prepare caramel sauce by placing the 1 cup of sugar in a heavy saucepan. Heat slowly, stirring constantly, until the sugar has melted and browned. Add boiling water slowly, stirring vigorously to avoid scorching. Cook until the mixture is syrupy and smooth. Remove saucepan from heat, still stirring, add the heavy cream. Drizzle over cooled pie in desired amount. Remainder can be served on the side.

HUNGARIAN APPLE PIE

2 ¼ cups sifted flour
¼ tsp. salt
½ tsp. double-acting baking powder
½ cup vanilla sugar
¾ cup cold butter
2 egg yolks, cold
1 tsp. lemon zest
3 medium green cooking apples
2 tsp. lemon juice
1 tsp. lemon zest
½ cup sugar
½ tsp. cinnamon
½ cup chopped walnuts
2 egg whites
Salt
2 T. breadcrumbs
1 whole egg, lightly beaten

Add first 4 dry ingredients to a large mixing bowl and stir together. Make a well in the center and add the butter, egg yolks and lemon zest. Working quickly, work all ingredients together until evenly mixed. Try to squeeze everything into a smooth ball. If too crumbly, add a little ice water to bind together. Try to prevent butter from softening. Flatten dough with the heel of your hand to create a disc, then fold edges into center and make a ball again. Wrap in plastic and chill. When ready to make pastry shell, allow to return to room temperature for a half hour. Divide the dough in half. Chill the smaller portion again. Preheat oven to 400 degrees Fahrenheit. Roll out the larger portion of pie crust to ¼ inch thick. Butter a 9" pie pan and place pie crust in. Trim to fit. Prick in several places with fork. Place in preheated oven to bake for 10 minutes, then remove and cool before filling.

Remove smaller portion of pie crust from refrigerator and allow to warm to room temperature. Prepare filling by peeling the apples, then grate them on the largest hole of a box grater. Immediately sprinkle with lemon juice and stir to prevent the apples from browning. Flavor apples with lemon zest cinnamon, ¼ cup of the sugar. Stir in the chopped nuts.

Roll out the remaining portion of piecrust. Preheat oven to 400 degrees Fahrenheit. In a separate mixing bowl, beat egg whites with a pinch of salt, then gradually add the remaining sugar and continue beating until stiff. Fold into the apple mixture. Sprinkle baked pie shell with breadcrumbs, then fill with apple mixture. Carefully put the upper crust into place, seal edges and prick the top with a fork. Paint the crust with beaten egg and place the pie in the middle of the oven to bake for 20 minutes or until top is a shiny golden brown.

OLD TIMEY CIDER PIE

1 recipe pate brisee
2/3 cup cornstarch
1 1/3 cups sugar
1 tsp. cinnamon
½ tsp. nutmeg
5 cups apple cider
1 cup heavy cream
¼ cup sugar
1 tsp. vanilla
½ cup chopped hickory or black walnuts

Prepare pate brisee and line a 9 inch pie plate. Prick with fork all over. Line bottom with parchment paper and fill with rice or dried beans to blind bake the shell. Bake shell in a preheated 400 degree Fahrenheit oven for 10 minutes. Remove beans or rice and parchment paper and continue to bake for another 10 to 15 minutes. Pie shell should be golden brown. Remove from oven and cool.

To prepare filling, in a large heavy saucepan, stir together the cornstarch, sugar, cinnamon and nutmeg. Over a medium heat, pour apple cider into sugar mixture in a stream, constantly stirring. Bring cider to a boil. Simmer the mixture, stirring, until it is thick and clear. Reduce heat to low and continue cooking for approximately 15 minutes. Pour filling into a bowl and cover with buttered wax paper or plastic wrap and cool to lukewarm. Pour filling into baked pie shell and allow it to continue to cool to room temperature.

Whip cream until lightly stiff, add sugar and vanilla. When fully stiff, spread over pie. Sprinkle with nuts.

BERRIES

I am in Lavinia Cooper's kitchen sitting on a vinyl turquoise blue chair with chrome legs and back. The most comfortable kitchen chair I have ever encountered. Lavinia has six of them that match her turquoise blue topped kitchen table. Lavinia is seventy-eight years young. Her bright blue eyes light up a suntanned face. Her gray hair stylishly frames her face which is barretted on each side. She has lived in the same home for sixty years. Her daughter, Ruthie, lives with her as well as her older brother Harlan and her sister-in-law Melba.

Mizz Cooper, what type of pies are you entering in the contest? I asked.

"Well, I am entering this here raspberry pie, a huckleberry pie and a blackberry pie."

Do you grow your own berries? I mean, are all these from your personal garden?

"Only the raspberries, honey. Only the raspberries. The others, I get directly from the Lord's garden."

I don't understand.

"Well, the raspberries my husband planted years ago. He stuck some Latham raspberry canes in the backyard. We've grown those for many years. Every year, I cut them back and plant more canes. I have the red raspberries and I also have some golden ones that look just like a summer sunset. I stick some in the deep freeze every year and I can some to eat during the winter. The Lord provides me with plenty of huckleberries and blackberries. All I do is take my daughter Ruthie with me and some buckets and we find all the berries we need. We follow the roadside and the hedgerows where the blackberries grow. We walk in the woods and find huckleberry patches on the south-facing sunny dry knobs. You have to be mighty quick to pick those before the deer get to 'em first. You have to be mighty careful though when you do this. You have to watch for snakes. I'm always afraid of finding a rattler or a copperhead. One time, my stars, I was picking blackberries and stepped further in to reach some berries just beyond my reach. I glanced down and saw a big black snake alookin' at me.

You can imagine how quick I tried to get outta there! I know them snakes lay awaitin' in the berry bushes. They coil up in there waitin' for the birds, then they strike up. If it wuren't for them snakes, I guess the Lord's garden would have less berries for the takin'. I sure love the songbirds, but they sure like those berries as much as I do. Everywhere you look in the summer are big blackberry patches here. They can be the bane of your existence. They sprout up outta nowhere and in the worst places. I cain't rightfully tell you how many millions of scratches I've had from blackberry vines. Those things are right evil. They'll scratch up your arms and legs mighty bad. The thorns stick to your clothes sometimes and trap you. But I do love them berries. There ain't nothin' better than a blackberry cobbler, with vanilla ice cream, for a special summertime dessert."

Ruthie sauntered into the kitchen wearing a light cotton sleeveless shift. Her blond straight hair was hanging down in her face with one hand holding a strand. Although Ruthie is in her forties, she casts the appearance of a sullen angst-ridden teenager.

"Ruthie, honey, pull that hair away from your pretty face. Go put your barrettes in. I've told you before if you can't keep the hair outta your face, I'm taking you down to the beauty shop and git you a pixie cut!"

"No, Momma! You are not cuttin' my hair!" Ruthie smoothed another strand of hair and leaned against the kitchen counter. "Momma's makin' pies!"

"Yes, I am. Now go put in your barrettes before I do it myself!" Lavinia ordered, then sighed. "Lorda mercy, that child really gets to me sometimes." Ruthie straightened up and left the room.

"I am sorry. I am so sorry for her behavior. As you can see, she is a special child. She is a good person, but she's about a sandwich short of a picnic. Sometimes, I am so tested with her."

"Do you have any help for her?" This reporter asked.

"Honey, this whole house needs help. Ever since my husband died ten years ago, I had to take care of her by myself. We don't have an old folks home around here. That is why I take care of Harlan and Melba. After my husband died, my brother Harlan had a stroke. He's a widower and there's nobody to care for him. Then Melba came down sick and broke her hip. Melba was married to my husband's brother but he passed on. They had no children so she had no one to care for her. She never really got much better after she broke her hip and she's confined to her bed now. I'm the only one they have left. So, I collect a lot of food, can it, freeze it, dry it, whatever. Every tenth jar or package, I donate to Silent Springs Community Church. For I believe that someone may need it more than I. We can make do."

"Wow, that's admirable."

"Let me show you my pantry," Lavinia said proudly.

We both stood up and walked over to what looked like a bedroom. My eyes took in walls of shelves filled with fruits, vegetable, meats, eggs, all canned, pickled, preserved. It was a veritable personal grocery store. The fruits and vegetables all shone with a jewel-like quality in the mason jars.

"This is amazing, I really mean it. How is it that you created this?"

"Well, to make a long story short, I put these shelves up right after my husband died. My older children prepared us a fiftieth wedding anniversary party. They had all moved away. We're the only ones still living here. They wanted to come home for a big celebration. They wanted us to renew our vows. We didn't really think that was necessary, but we decided that we would go to church that morning and then after the service, the kids had rented the hall over by the volunteer fire department. We all went there. Had a nice barbeque, lots of fried chicken and potato salad. My oldest daughter baked a monstruous apple caramel cake that was my husband's favorite. We all had a wonderful time. Some of the boys played the fiddle and we danced the night away. It was just like a barn dance from a long time ago. The next day, my husband said he was tired. Just too much excitement from the day before, I thought. Although he checked on the cows and whatnot, he was movin' mighty slow. I spent the morning picking green beans and then prepared them. I started pickling green beans after lunch. At one point, I figured I'd check on him since things were pretty quiet around here. No TV on, no radio. It was mighty warm that day. And humid! The fan was in the livin' room winda but I wasn't gettin' any relief from it in the kitchen. The canning pot was a-boilin' away. I was slick with perspiration. My brow was beadin' up and the sweat rolled down into my eyeballs. They were a-burnin like all get-out! Lordy, all I could think about was to get them green beans done. The last thing I remembered he had been sittin' in his recliner. I came around the corner from the kitchen and saw he was still sittin' in his chair and all the color was drained from his face. I threw down my dishrag and ran over to check on his breathin'. I didn't see him breathin', couldn't feel a pulse, so I thought I'd start that CPR thing they taught us at the Volunteer Fire Department. I leaned over to blow some air into his mouth. I tried to kinda lock our lips together. He had a big wad of chaw stuck between his lip and his gums. My stars, that nasty stuff tasted terrible! I got it in my mouth and I yelled "Holy Shit!" Excuse me for that, but I cain't do it. He's gone and I cain't bring him back. I spit, spit, spit, but the taste of that chaw was too much. I had to let him go. As you can imagine, I wuren't too happy 'bout it plus it took me an extree day to finish them beans. I had to take care of the pending business.

So I was married to the man for fifty years and a half day then he left me. Well, I took our anniversary money and went on down to the lumber yard and bought me some boards. I thought, I gotta start hoardin' some food around here because there's no one to bring me home the bread and butter, if you know what I mean. So that's how this room came to be."

"It is pretty impressive, Mizz Cooper. I'm sorry for your loss."

"Well, I thank ya. To finish up my story, when he died, I called the operator and she called the County Coroner. That was a new thing. You just cain't call the mortuary anymore. They have to officially deem you dead, I guess. It was a big paperwork nightmare. I'll give you some good advice, don't ever die at home. Make sure you die in a hospital somewhere, it saves a lot of grief. Anyway, I was so busy with all them officials and what not, it was a couple of days before I could call my older kids to let them know their daddy died. It wouldn'ta mattered a hoot anyways. They were still on the road goin' home from our anniversary party. They were madder'n wet hens. All they could say was why didn't you call us? I did try callin' ya, you all were not home yet! Why this, why that. Well, I said, "The hell with y'all. Actin' like that, can you imagine? I haven't heard from them since. I am smart enough to know that when they are called and informed that I have passed on, they will zoom in trying to get every last cent. I am not goin' to let them come here, when I'm gone, like a bunch of turkey vultures. I had a will written out. I sold off all our acreage and just have postage-stamped my house and yard. All the money I earned from that is in the bank. Ruthie will inherit it all. I haven't touched it. I'll go down with the ship without touching a dime, if I have to. She will need everything I can spare. So that's why I created my pantry."

"Wow, again, Mizz Cooper! Let me ask you one question before I go with your entries and recipes. What made you want to enter the Prickleberrry Pie Contest?"

"Well, I don't rightly know. I think that deep down, I'm just a country woman, who lived as best she could. Dedicated her life to her family. Dedicated to faith in the Lord. Dedicated to keep her family, friends and strangers fed. When I go, I'll probably be not remembered for anything I did in my life. It would be nice, though, for people to remember me, just to say, "That woman could sure make a pie!"

LAVINIA'S` BLUEBERRY PIE

4 cups blueberries or huckleberries
1 cup sugar
4 T. flour
Pinch of salt
1 ½ T. lemon juice
1 recipe standard pastry
Milk
Sugar for sprinkling

Preheat oven to 450 degrees Fahrenheit. Prepare pastry crust and line a 9" pie pan. Mix washed berries with sugar, flour, salt and lemon juice. Pour berry mixture into pie crust and cover with top crust. Brush with milk, then sprinkle with sugar.

Bake in 450 degree oven for 10 minutes, then reduce heat to 350 degrees Fahrenheit and bake 30 minutes longer.

Variations:
Substitute 2 T. quick-cooking tapioca for the flour in the berry mixture. Add ½ tsp. cinnamon or allspice to the berry mixture.

BLACKBERRY PIE

3 cups fresh ripe blackberries
1 cup sugar
2 T. flour
2 T. lemon juice
Pinch of salt
1 recipe standard pie crust
1 pat of butter

Preheat oven to 450 degrees Fahrenheit. Line 9" pie pan with pastry crust. In mixing bowl, combine blackberries, sugar, flour, lemon juice and salt. Pour into prepared pie pan. Take pat of butter and break into small pies, dotting the pie filling. Cover with top crust and crimp edge well.

Bake for 10 minutes, then reduce heat to 350 degrees Fahrenheit and continue baking for 30 minutes longer.

Variation:
Substitute blackberries with boysenberries, youngberries, loganberries, marionberries or tayberries.

BUMBLEBERRY PIE

2 large cooking apples
1 cup chopped fresh rhubarb
1 cup fresh raspberries
1 cup fresh blueberries
1 cup fresh blackberries
1 cup fresh strawberries, halved
1 cup sugar
1 T. lemon juice
1 recipe standard pie crust

Preheat oven to 450 degrees Fahrenheit. Prepare pie crusts and line a 9" pie pan. Peel, core, and chop the apples. Place in a large mixing bowl. Add the rhubarb and all the berries. Stir in the sugar, flour and lemon juice. Stir gently. Pour into prepared pan.

Take remaining pie crust, slip into strips and create a lattice crust. Fold edges under and crimp well.

Bake for 15 minutes, then reduce heat to 350 degrees Fahrenheit and bake for an additional 30 minutes.

BERRY AND PEACH PIE

2 cups fresh peeled, pitted and sliced peaches
2 cups blueberries or blackberries
1 cup sugar
1 ½ T. quick-cooking tapioca
Pinch of salt
1 recipe southern or cream cheese pastry

Preheat oven to 425 degrees Fahrenheit. Prepare pastry and line a 9" pie pan. In medium bowl, mix the sugar, tapioca and salt. In a large mixing bowl, add the fruit, then carefully stir in the sugar mixture. Pour into prepared pie pan. Bake for ten minutes, then reduce heat to 350 degrees Fahrenheit and continue baking for another 30 minutes. Crust should be lightly browned.

CRANBERRY PIE

4 cups fresh cranberries
1 ½ cups sugar
2 T. flour
Pinch of salt
3 T. water
1 T. butter
1 recipe standard pie crust

Preheat oven to 450 degrees Fahrenheit. Prepare pie crusts and line a 9" pie pan. Rinse cranberries and remove any stems, twigs or leaves. Chop coarsely and in a large mixing bowl, add with sugar, flour, salt, water and butter. Pour filling into prepared pie pan. Form lattice top, folding edges under and crimp well. Bake for 15 minutes, then reduce heat to 350 degrees Fahrenheit and continuing baking for another 30 minutes.

Variation:

Substitute the 3 T. water with orange juice and add 1 tsp. of orange zest.

CRANBERRY APPLE PIE

1 ½ cups fresh cranberries
1 ½ cups diced cooking apples
½ cup water
1 cup sugar
1 recipe standard pie crust

Preheat oven to 450 degrees Fahrenheit. Prepare pie crusts. Line a 9" pie pan with pastry and prepare top for lattice crust. In large saucepan, on medium heat, cook cranberries and apples in the ½ cup water until tender. Add sugar and stir until melted. Remove from heat and cool slightly. Pour into prepared pie pan and cover with a lattice crust.

Bake for 10 minutes, then reduce heat to 350 degrees Fahrenheit and continue baking for 30 minutes longer.

RASPBERRY RHUBARB PIE

1/3 cup flour
4 cups sliced rhubarb
2 cups raspberries
1 ¼ cups sugar
Juice of a half lemon
1 T. sweet butter, cut into small pieces
Milk or cream
Sugar for sprinkling
1 recipe pate brisee

Preheat oven to 375 degrees Fahrenheit. Prepare pate brisee. Line a 9" pie pan with pastry and prepare remainder for a lattice crust.

In a medium mixing bowl, combine flour and sugar. In a large mixing bowl, combine the rhubarb and raspberries. Add the lemon juice. Sprinkle in the sugar/flour mixture and stir gently to coat the rhubarb. Avoid crushing the raspberries. Pour into prepared pie pan, dot with butter chips.

Cover top with lattice crust. Brush with milk or cream and sprinkle on sugar.

Place in oven and bake for 1 hour.

FRESH STRAWBERRY PIE

1 cup sugar
2 T. cornstarch
Pinch of salt
3 cups fresh strawberries
1 T. sweet butter
1 recipe standard pie crust

Preheat oven to 450 degrees Fahrenheit. Prepare pie crust and line a 8" pie pan. Wash strawberries, trim tops off and quarter. Place in large mixing bowl. In a separate bowl, mix the sugar, cornstarch and salt. Add to the strawberries. Pour mixture into prepared pie pan, dot with butter chips and cover with top crust. Crimp edge well.

Bake for 10 minutes, then reduce heat to 350 degrees Fahrenheit and continue baking for another 30 minutes.

Variation:
Substitute the strawberries for raspberries in same amount.

STRAWBERRY RHUBARB PIE

¼ cup flour
1 ¼ cups sugar
¼ tsp. ground nutmeg
1 cup fresh strawberries
2 cups diced rhubarb
2 T. butter
1 recipe standard pie crust

Preheat oven to 425 degrees Fahrenheit. Prepare pie crust and line a 9" pie pan. In a small bowl, combine the flour, sugar and nutmeg.

Wash and trim strawberries. If they are large, slice them into quarters or disks. In a large mixing bowl, toss the strawberries with the rhubarb. Pour 3/4s of the flour/sugar mixture into the fruit and mix well.

Pour remaining flour/sugar mixture into prepared pie pan. Pour fruit on top. Dot with butter chips. Create lattice top and crimp edge well.

Bake for 10 minutes, then reduce heat to 350 degrees Fahrenheit and continue baking for an additional 30 minutes.

OLD FASHIONED GOOSEBERRY PIE

3 cups gooseberries
1 cup sugar
½ cup water
2 T. flour
½ cup sugar
Pinch of salt
1 tsp. cinnamon
½ tsp. allspice
Pinch of nutmeg
1 T. butter
1 recipe standard pie crust

Preheat oven to 450 degrees Fahrenheit. Prepare pie crust and line a 9" pie pan. In a small mixing bowl, combine ½ cup sugar, flour, salt and spices. Stir to mix well. In medium saucepan, cook gooseberries,

1 cup of sugar and the ½ cup of water on medium heat. Cook until berries are tender, then remove from heat. Add the sugar/flour mixture to the berries and stir well, incorporating all the ingredients.

Pour filling into prepared pie pan and dot with butter chips. Cover with top crust, crimping edge well.

Bake for 10 minutes, then reduce heat to 350 degrees Fahrenheit and bake for another 30 minutes.

CREAM AND CUSTARD

"Hey there! I am Maryann Fox. My husband, Ronnie, and I own and operate Smiling Cow Dairy, glad you could come on over" she said as she walked out of the barn carrying a shiny stainless steel bucket. Despite the morning's heat, she was wearing a flannel shirt, blue jeans and wellington boots up to her knees.

"Nice to meet ya!" this reporter said. "Aren'tcha hot wearing all that get-up?"

"Well, I'm used to it now. When you own a dairy farm, the cows come first. We've been in the barn since 4:30 this morning. It's kinda cool then, so I dress warm. I can always peel later," she smiled. "Come on in and I'll give you the pies to take."

We walked towards her white clapboard farmhouse and into the kitchen where the screen door banged shut. Everything was as neat as a pin and white. White walls, white cabinets, white table and chairs, you get the picture.

"Wow! Everything is white in here. Do you just like white or is there a reason?"

Maryann laughed. "It is kind of a family joke. I always say it is milk white because we are a dairy farm. Ronnie contradicts me and says it is snow white and don't ever forget it."

"How so?"

"Well, to make a long story short, Ronnie and I are the new kids on the block. We moved here twenty-two years ago. We both grew up on farms, fell in love, got married, started a family and bought some pasturage next to my parents' farm. We were young, probably stupid, but we started a dairy farm. It was rough going at first but we struggled and we worked through the difficulties. We had three little ones, all a year apart, stair-stepping. Then one fall, it got real cold, real fast. Ronnie hadn't finished putting the hay in the barn and he ran out of time. The snow was starting to come down and it wasn't even Halloween yet. In his rush to lay the bales in, he must have gotten careless. He had a tractor accident and broke his leg in three places. I'll spare you the details. Anyhow, my dad and uncles finished up for us. Ronnie was laid up pretty bad. That left little old me to handle the chores. It snowed, kept snowing and snowed some more."

"Huh? Are we talking about the Ozarks, because I never heard of that kind of weather here. I mean we've had ice and snow but it doesn't last long."

"Oh sorry. I must have forgotten to tell you. This was Wisconsin." Maryann apologized.

"I thought I must be getting confused. Now I realize that. It confirms my thoughts that you were not originally from here. I don't hear that twangy drawl people speak around here in your voice."

Yes, that's right. I never lost that mid-west hardness in the consonants. Anyhow, to finish up on my story, Ronnie was casted up to his hip in bed nice and toasty warm while I ran the farm. All the chores, everything, plus I still had to come in and take care of the kids and him. It snowed for four months straight. I was out in storms and blizzards chasing down cows, fixing broken water lines that had froze up, fixing fence lines, fixing milking machines, calving, getting frost-bit, you name it. By the spring thaw, I was plum exhausted. I hadn't realized it at first but I was expecting again, this time with twins. Ronnie was on crutches for months and as we eased out of summer I started getting anxious. I couldn't do a repeat. We had five babies now and I was worn thin. I'm sure Ronnie had felt guilty laying there day after day and though he said he was sorry, he told me that he would make it up to me. Hah, I thought. Then one day, he told me that he was going on a hunting trip. I said to him 'What??? You are not going hunting. You are NOT going to shoot your foot and lay in bed here for another four months, no way Jose!'

As it turned out, my little brother Melvin had graduated college that June with a degree in agriculture and animal husbandry. Ronnie had talked him into running the farm in his stead. By hook or by crook, Ronnie was going on his hunting trip. And he did. I spent the next two weeks teaching Melvin everything there was to know about our farm. While they may teach you a lot in college, they don't hit the practical applications. Well, maybe they did and Melvin didn't pick up on them. Surprisingly, he never really did absorb what Mom and Dad did on the family farm while we were growing up. He was totally oblivious.

Too bad Dad hadn't been harder with him early on, it would have been so much easier for me.

When Ronnie came home, he brought all of us a few gifts and then handed me a packet of papers. 'Here's your new farm,' he told me. 'No snow anymore.' I looked through it, saw the diagrams, read the legal description and then realized we were moving far far away. Prior to his departure, he had arranged the sale of our farm with my dad and brother. Melvin never said a word to me. Nor Mom and Dad.

While I was sad to leave my family, I knew it was really time to fly the coop. We'd see them for the big holidays anyway but one guarantee was that I didn't have to live in the frozen north. 'Ronnie', I said, 'you really put the pressure on now. First of all, we are moving to Arkansas. There is no help from our family. We'll have no one in case of emergencies. Secondly, the expectations are extremely high. We're from Wisconsin, known for our dairies. What would people say if we failed? We're cheeseheads!'

So, twenty-two years later, I can say we were successful. Farmed more acreage than we had before, have more cows than we could have imagined. Maintained a great reputation, won numerous awards for our milk and other dairy products, raised our kids, all with college educations and all live close by. A very happy life here, I'll never complain. I love it here. So does Ronnie and the kids. One rule we always told our kids was to remember your roots. Your roots genetically make you into who you are. So if my kitchen is snow white, so be it. I came from the snow and I won't forget. I'll live in my milk white kitchen on my dairy farm, pure as the driven snow. Now let me get you those pies!"

THE BASIC FARM STYLE CREAM PIE

1/3 cup sugar
3 T. cornstarch
Pinch of salt
½ cup cold milk
1/1/2 cups scalding milk
3 egg yolks, beaten until light yellow
1 ½ tsp. vanilla
1 baked pie shell of your choice
Meringue

In top of a double boiler, mix sugar, cornstarch and salt, add the cold milk and blend well. Then, over medium heat, gradually add the scalding milk in a stream, stirring constantly. Mixture will thicken. Temper egg yolks by adding a small amount of the hot pudding mixture and stirring well. Add egg yolk mixture beating rapidly to hot pudding and cook 2-3 minutes longer. Add vanilla. Remove from heat and allow to cool.

Preheat oven to 350 degrees Fahrenheit. Pour into prepared pie pan. Smooth filling. Add meringue to the top making decorative peaks and swirls. Place in hot oven, watching closely. Meringue tips will begin to turn golden brown. When meringue no longer has "raw" look, remove from oven and cool.

Variations:

Almond Cream – substitute the vanilla with 1 tsp. almond extract. Top meringue with ¼ cup sliced almonds. Bake until the almonds are toasted, then remove from oven.

THE PRICKLEBERRY PIE CONTEST

Banana Cream – slice 4 bananas. On bottom of pie shell, lay half the banana slices then cover with half of the pudding filling. Top second half of pudding with remaining bananas. Top with meringue and brown as directed. Rather than topping with meringue, top with sweetened whipped cream and chill.

Chocolate Cream – Chop 4 ounces of bittersweet chocolate. Add to scalding milk to melt completely. Proceed with recipe as directed.

Coconut Cream–Stir 1 ½ cups of moist shredded coconut into hot filling. Top meringue with ¼ cup moist shredded coconut. Bake until coconut is lightly toasted, then remove from oven and cool.

Date Cream Pie – Stir in 1 cup chopped dates into filling. Dates should be of high quality, moist.

Espresso Cream – Prepare chocolate wafer crust for this pie. Add 2 T. espresso powder to the sugar, cornstarch and salt mixture. Proceed as above. When adding the vanilla, include ¼ cup coffee liqueur. Top the pie with sweetened whipped cream. Sprinkle with dark chocolate covered espresso beans. Chill.

Mango Cream – Slice 1 ripe mango and cut into ½" dice. Add fruit to cooled filling.

Orange Cream – Drain an 8 ounce can of mandarin oranges and add to the filling. Add ½ tsp. of orange zest to meringue and bake as directed.

Peaches and Cream–Place filling into pie shell as directed above. Top filling with sliced sweetened peaches. Replace meringue with sweetened whipped cream and chill.

Pineapple Cream – Stir in 1 ½ cups drained crushed pineapple into filling and proceed as above.

Raspberry – Add 1 cup raspberries to cooled filling and proceed as above.

Rum Raisin Cream Pie – Two hours before preparing pie, soak ½ cup seedless raisins in ¼ cup dark rum. Add raisins to cooled filling.

Strawberries and Cream – Top filling with 1 cup sliced sweetened strawberries, then cover with sweetened whipped cream. Chill.

COUNTRY BUTTERMILK PIE

1 ½ cups sugar
1 T. flour
3 eggs, slightly beaten
1 stick sweet butter, melted
¾ cup buttermilk
1 tsp. vanilla
½ tsp. almond extract
1 9" pie crust

Preheat oven to 400 degrees Fahrenheit. Mix flour with sugar, then add the slightly beaten eggs and melted butter. Add buttermilk, vanilla and almond extract. Mix well. Pour into unbaked pie crust. Bake for 15 minutes, then reduce heat to 325 degrees Fahrenheit and continue baking for 35 minutes. Remove from oven and cool. Pie should be served at room temperature.

Variation:
Substitute vanilla and almond extract for 1 tsp. lemon extract.
Substitute vanilla and almond extract with zest of 1 lemon, 1 T. lemon juice. Stir in well.

BUTTERSCOTCH PIE

¾ cup brown sugar, packed

¼ cup sugar
1/3 cup flour
2 cups scalded milk
Pinch of salt
3 egg yolks, beaten
1 ½ T. sweet butter
1 tsp. vanilla
1 baked pie shell
Meringue, using 3 egg whites, beat until just stiff. Sprinkle with a teaspoon of sugar, and beat until stiff.

Combine both types of sugar with the flour and salt, mix well. Add the hot scalded milk to the dry mixture slowly in a stream, stirring constantly. Cook in top of double boiler stirring occasionally until thickened. This should take approximately 15 minutes. Temper the egg yolks by adding small amount of the hot filling and stirring rapidly, then stir egg yolks into the hot mixture. Constantly beating, continue for about 2 minutes. Add the butter, still stirring, until it has melted. Let mixture cool, then add vanilla. Pour into pie crust and smooth over. Top with meringue creating peaks and swirls. Bake in a preheated 425 degree Fahrenheit oven. Watch closely as meringue begins to brown, then remove when it has reached the golden color you are seeking.

EXTRA RICH BUTTERSCOTCH PIE

¼ cup sweet butter
1 cup packed brown sugar
1 ¼ whole milk, divided
½ cup heavy whipping cream
1 egg
1 egg yolk
3 T. cornstarch 1 tsp. double strength vanilla
Pate brisee crust
Meringue made with brown sugar

On medium heat, melt butter in a medium saucepan. Add the brown sugar and stir. Sugar should melt. Continue to cook and stir until smooth. Whisk in ¾ cup of the milk and the whipping cream, stir constantly until it comes to a boil. Remove from heat.

Preheat oven to 425 degrees Fahrenheit. In a medium bowl, whisk together egg, egg yolk and the remaining milk. Add the cornstarch and salt, then add to hot mixture. Cook over medium heat until the mixture thickens. This should take approximately 5 minutes. Stir in vanilla. Pour into prepared pie shell and smooth over. Top with meringue, creating peak and swirls for a decorative finish. Bake in hot oven 3-5 minutes or until is a light golden brown.

CHOCOLATE CREAM PIE

1 ¼ cups sugar
1/3 cup cornstarch
Pinch of salt
3 cups milk
3 ounces (3 squares) unsweetened chocolate
4 egg yolks, slightly beaten
1 T. vanilla
Meringue or Sweetened Whipped Cream
1 prepared 9" pie shell

In a heavy saucepan, combine sugar, cornstarch and salt. While stirring constantly, over medium-low heat, pour in milk slowly in a stream. When smooth, add chocolate. Allow to melt and continue stirring until mixture comes to a boil. Temper egg yolks by taking small amount of hot mixture and mixing in well, then add back to the hot chocolate mixture Reduce heat to low and let mixture thicken, about 2-3 minutes. Remove from heat, stir in vanilla. Pour into pie shell.

Preheat oven to 425 degrees Fahrenheit. Top the pie with prepared meringue, creating peaks and swirls. Bake in hot oven for 3-5 minutes until the meringue is lightly browned. Cool slightly, then chill for at least 2 hours before serving.

If you prefer a whipped cream topping instead of meringue, when you pour filling into pie shell, cover with plastic wrap and chill at least 2 hours. Spread pie with sweetened whipped cream.

CHOCOLATE RUM PIE

½ cup milk
½ cup heavy whipping cream
6 squares semisweet chocolate
3 egg yolks
¼ cup sugar
Pinch of salt
1/3 cup light rum
3 egg whites
3 T. sugar
1 T. powdered sugar
1 tsp. light rum
1 baked pie shell
Prepare 8" pie shell. Bake and cool.

In top of double boiler with simmering water, heat milk and cream. Stir until mixture has scalded, then add chocolate. Stir to assure that it melts completely. In a medium mixing bowl, combine egg yolks, the ¼ cup sugar and the salt. Beat until light and fluffy. Add the chocolate mixture in a thin stream, continue to beat constantly, until well blended.

Transfer the chocolate mixture to the top of double boiler. Cook over simmering water, stirring constantly, until thick and smooth. Remove from heat and stir in the 1/3 cup light rum. Allow to cool, then chill.

Beat egg whites in a small bowl until foamy. Slowly beat in the remaining 3 T. sugar until meringue becomes stiff and glossy. Fold meringue into chilled chocolate mixture. Pour into prepared pie shell, smooth top, then chill. Beat heavy cream with the powdered sugar and teaspoon of rum until stiff. Decoratively pipe on top of pie. Chill pie for approximately 4 hours before serving. This will assure that the filling has set.

CHERRY CREAM CHEESE PIE

2 small packages cream cheese
½ pint whipping cream
½ cup powdered sugar
1 tsp. vanilla
1 can cherry pie filling
1 9" graham cracker crust

In medium size mixing bowl, allow cream cheese to reach room temperature. When soft, beat until smooth and creamy. In a separate mixing bowl, beat whipping cream until partially stiff, then add sugar. Beat until stiff. Add whipped cream to the cream cheese and blend well. Add the vanilla and stir in well. Pour into prepared pie shell and chill. When cold, top with cherry pie filling.

MAPLE CREAM PIE

3 large eggs
2 cups pure dark amber maple syrup
1 cup heavy cream
3 T. flour
2 cups sweetened whipped cream
1 baked pie shell

Preheat oven to 375 degrees Fahrenheit. In a medium bowl, beat eggs. Add maple syrup, cream and flour. Whisk until well blended, then pour into prepared pie shell.

Bake for 40-50 minutes. Pie should be puffed up and golden. Let cool. Decorate with whipped cream and chill at least an hour before serving.

OLD FASHIONED CUSTARD PIE

4 eggs, slightly beaten
¼ tsp. salt
½ cup sugar
3 cups milk, scalded
½ tsp. vanilla
Nutmeg
½ recipe standard pie crust

Preheat oven to 450 degree Fahrenheit. In a large mixing bowl, combine eggs, salt and sugar, while stirring constantly, add milk in a thin stream, then add vanilla. Pour filling into pie shell. Sprinkle with nutmeg. Bake for 10 minutes, then reduce heat to 325 degrees Fahrenheit and continue baking for approximately 35 minutes or until knife inserted in center comes out clean.

Variations:
Caramel – Place the ½ cup in a small saucepan and over medium heat, allow sugar to melt and caramelize. Stir into scalded milk before combining it with the egg mixture. Bake as directed above.
Coconut – Add 1 cup moist shredded coconut to custard before baking.

TRANSPARENT CUSTARD PIE

2 cups sugar

4 T. butter, melted
3 T. cream
4 egg yolks, beaten
½ tsp. salt
1 T. flour
1 tsp. vanilla
½ recipe standard pie crust
1 recipe brown sugar meringue

Preheat oven to 450 degrees Fahrenheit. Line pie pan with pastry crust. Mix sugar, butter and cream together. Add egg yolks, salt, flour and vanilla. Pour into prepared pie shell.

Bake in hot oven for 10 minutes, then reduce heat to 350 degrees Fahrenheit and continue baking for 30 minutes or until a knife inserted in center comes out clean. Increase oven temperature to 425 degrees Fahrenheit.

Cover pie with brown sugar meringue, creating peaks and swirls. Bake in hot oven for 3-5 minutes until meringue turns golden brown.

PEANUT BUTTER CUSTARD PIE

1 ½ cups milk
½ cup heavy cream
1 package vanilla pudding mix
1/3 cup creamy peanut butter
¼ cup finely chopped peanuts
½ cup heavy whipping cream
2 tsp. sugar
1 tsp. vanilla
Chopped peanuts
1 prepared pie shell*

In medium saucepan, pour in pudding mix. Over medium heat, while stirring constantly, gradually add milk and cream. Mixture should be smooth. Heat until it reaches a full rolling boil. Remove from heat and add peanut butter, stirring until smooth. Add ¼ cup finely chopped peanuts. Pour into prepared crust. Chill until firm, about 4 hours.

For topping, Beat ½ cup heavy whipping cream with 2 tsp. sugar. Whip until stiff. Add the vanilla. Spread onto pie in a decorative fashion.

*You can use a standard pie crust or prepare by finely crushing 3 cups of ready to eat puffed chocolate or peanut butter flavored cereal. This should yield approximately ¾ cup of crumbs. Add to the crumbs ½ cup finely chopped peanuts and 6 T. melted butter. Press mixture onto sides and bottom of a 9" pie pan. Chill for 1 hour before preparing the pie filling.

AMISH VANILLA PIES

1 cup sugar
4 T. flour
1 egg, well beaten
1 cup molasses
2 cups water
1 tsp. vanilla
2 cups flour
1 cup brown sugar
1 tsp. cream of tartar
1 tsp. baking soda
¼ cup butter, soft
¼ cup lard
2 pie shells, unbaked

Preheat oven to 350 degrees Fahrenheit. In a large saucepan, combine the first 6 ingredients in the order given. Bring to a full rolling boil, remove from heat and set aside to cool.

In a large mixing bowl, combine the next 6 ingredients and rub them together with your fingers to make crumbs.

Pour half of the cooked filling into each of the prepared pie shells. Cover each pie with the crumbs. Bake for 45 minutes.

PUDDING PIE

5 beaten eggs
2 heaping T. of flour
4 T. sugar
Pinch of salt
3 cups milk
1 tsp. vanilla or lemon extract
Shredded coconut, if desired

Preheat oven to 350 degrees Fahrenheit. Combine all the ingredients and stir well. Check to make sure you have enough flavoring. Grease an 8" or 9" pie pan. Pour mixture into pan. Sprinkle with coconut, if desired.

Bake at 350 degrees Fahrenheit until done. Insert a knife or toothpick into center of pie. If it comes out clean, custard pie is done. This recipe is over 250 years old. It makes it's own crust.

FRIED PIES

Danise Childress just finished making her bed with military precision. She had done this every morning for as long as she could remember. She took her damp wash cloth that she had used in her shower that same morning and wiped the dust from her bedroom suite, then dropped it down the laundry chute in the hallway. Her husband was at work already at the electric company and her youngest daughter,

Tawny, was downstairs in the kitchen helping her meemaw eat her breakfast.

Danise, looked around her bedroom and saw with motherly eyes the pictures of her family looking back. She was suffering a little bit from the empty nest syndrome still. Tawny was home on summer break from her first year of college. Danise and Chuck, her husband of twenty-eight years, had a pretty good comfortable but modest life. The last six months though has been quite a rollercoaster ride. Danise's mother, Elsie, had come to live with them. Elsie had old-timer's disease and it was late stage. Not a single sibling had any more strength to take care of her. Whether it was a lack of patience, tolerance, or just selfishness, no one wanted the old woman anymore. Danise and Chuck took her in and tried to make the best of it. It irked Danise. The old woman was truly frustrating. She was more childlike than Danise's kids had ever been. Chuck treated her as major entertainment. He couldn't wait to see what she would do next. He couldn't understand why Danise would become so upset with the little things the old woman did. Little did he realize that Danise secretly feared she would end up in the same condition.

Danise sat on the side of her bed as she did every morning and cracked open the Daily 365 Bible to read today's portion. "I just don't understand this…" she said to herself. She read the passage over several times but could not comprehend any meaning that she could apply to her life. "Why do I need to know who begat who? How does that help my life? Damn!" She slammed the book closed which sounded like a slap as simultaneously the front door bell rang.

"I'll get it." She yelled, walking down the stairs to the front door. As she approached the entryway, she heard Tawny and her mother talking in the kitchen, followed by clanging of pots and pans.

She opened the door and found Pastor Wilkes on the stoop. "Come on in, Pastor!" She said with a guilty look on her face. Just moments before she had slapped the Bible shut. Could he have heard that, she asked herself. "And what can I do for you this fine day?"

"Well, Danise, Ah was drivin' down the road this mornin' and when ah saw your house, ah thought ah'd stop in. Ah hope you don't mind."

"I really hate to admit this, but you probably heard me say a bad word just moments ago. Maybe the Lord heard my prayer. Come in and sit a few moments. Can I get you some coffee?" She asked sheepishly.

"Is there anythin' botherin' you? Do you want to tell me about it?" He asked cautiously.

"I am not a person who complains, Pastor. I take things pretty well. Maybe what's got my goat this morning is just trivial. Not worth talking about."

"There's nothin' considered trivial. Think of a grain of sand: One grain. But when the wind blows in another grain and then another, if the floor is not swept, before too long, you have a dune. Handle your small cares as they come in lieu of waitin' for a crisis, praise the Lord! Remember the parable of the mustard seed. So what can ah he'p you with today?"

"This!" Danise answered holding her Daily 365 Bible in the air. "I have read this four years in a row. Four years in a row! I still don't understand it. I still don't get answers sometimes. I feel guilty and unworthy. Why don't I feel enlightened? It makes me feel sad and mad that I don't see solutions to my needs sometimes. Do you know how some people at bible study talk about an issue and suddenly someone will spout a verse or passage that makes sense that gives an answer? I'm amazed at those people. They draw instantly from their memory. I can't do that. Some days I feel like I can't retain anything."

"Danise, the Lord works in mysterious ways. You have many wonderful qualities. Don't count yourself short. While you may have studied the Bible most of your life, you certainly have faith. You certainly understan' the Lord and our Church. Maybe you try too hard to find meanin' in somethin' that is really just a historical record. There are times when we all should just accept something without asking why? The ways of God in some ways is just mysterious. Who are we to ask? Was there somethin' in today's readin' that you had difficulty with?" He asked honestly and sincerely.

"Yes," she said as she reopened the Bible to today's offering. "Read this! What does this possess or attribute to my life today?" Her finger pointing and hitting the verses. Danise reached out offering the good book to the pastor.

He took it and read the passage, smiling. "No, I can agree with you on today's passage. The importance is just that you have read it. The Lord doesn't ask you to soak up every word, nor does he demand you memorize every word. Don't worry Danise, there is nothin' wrong with you and there is no shame in not understandin' everythin'. Perhaps some day this passage may mean somethin' to 'ya. Today's selection dealt with providing lineage. Think on it."

"Well, that's good news, I will." She answered and smiled. "Can I still offer you a cup of coffee? I didn't mean to trouble you. In fact, I guess it was a blessing you stopped by. I feel better now."

"No, I'm fine, really. Ah'm glad ah could offer some comfort." He said as he raised his hand into a stop position and shifted position in his chair.

"Mom? Momma?" Danise heard Tawny call her from the kitchen. The clanging and banging from the kitchen was getting pretty distracting.

"What, hon?" Danise answered. "Can you excuse me for a minute, Pastor?" She rushed into the kitchen to find her mother, Elsie, working at the kitchen table. There were mixing bowls, a flour canister and various measuring cups laid out. Peaches and syrup were boiling away in a shiny saucepan on the stove.

"Charlene, pass me the sugar canister, will you?" Elsie asked.

"Momma, I'm not Charlene, I'm Danise."

"Charlene, Danise, it doesn't matter which daughter you are. Just pass me that sugar, will you, honey?" Elsie asked. She was bent over the kitchen table and her shaky right arm extended backwards trying to clutch a pass of sugar.

Danise passed her the sugar. "What's happening in here?"

"Mom, Meemaw says she is making fried pies. We heard on the radio that there is a pie contest in Silent Springs. Meemaw is entering the contest. She already called the number. A lady will be picking up the fried pies later this afternoon."

"That's right", Elsie nodding her head. "This was your brother John Dale's favorite dee-zert. He could eat a hun-nert of 'em! He'd be so excited when I fried them up. My, he loved them so. You remember that, Danise?"

Tawny looked at her mother with a quizzical smile. "Do you think she will really do it?"

"I don't know, honey. She just kind of came alive today. We'll see." Danise returned to the living room to find the Pastor still sitting peacefully in the armchair. Thinking to herself that the kitchen already looked like a disaster area, she started to mentally gear up the possibility that she would need to super clean up once the old lady was done, especially if some lady was coming to pick up the pies. Wouldn't want a stranger to see and think that they lived in a cluttered pig sty.

"Is everything alright?" He asked.

"I guess so, I don't know. My mother is making pies. She heard about the pie contest and wants to enter it. The funny thing is that she's sat quiet about for the last two weeks. Now today, she is a bundle of energy and she even looks thirty years younger right now! She is so focused on her pies. It's kind of amazing!"

"Well, in that case, ah'll take my leave. As ah said earlier, Danise, the Lord works in mysterious ways. Watch her closely today. Ah've heard of Alzheimer patients catching their kitchens on fire, forgetting the oven glove on the burners, stuff like that. Keep the faith, my friend. And…Keep your eyes open."

"Thanks for stopping by," Danise said as she led him to the front door.

She let the pastor out and shut the door, leaning briefly against it.

"Lord, give me the strength!" She mumbled and walked into the kitchen.

"Mother, you haven't made fried pies since I was a girl. I sure loved it too when you did. You made the best pies I ever tasted." Danise said as she hugged her mother's side.

"Tawny, can you help Meemaw for a while? There is something I need to do upstairs. She looked at Tawny, tall and thin, her flaxen hair bound into a bouncy ponytail.

"Yes, Mom." A second passed by, "Mom? Mom?" Tawny asked.

"Yes?"

THE PRICKLEBERRY PIE CONTEST

"Don't you think it's great Meemaw is making pies today?" Tawny mouthed almost silently.

Danise smiled and bobbed her head up and down. "Yes, I do."

Danise bounded up the stairs to her bedroom and shut the door. She called Chuck on the phone and explained to him what had happened this morning. Her mother has had a transformation overnight. She was making fried pies, peach and apple. It was like she had stepped back in time.

MEEMAW'S FRIED APPLE PIES

1 cup shortening
3 cups flour
1 egg, slightly beaten
½ cup water
1 tsp. salt
1 tsp. vinegar
8 ounces dried apples

1 cup sugar
1 tsp. cinnamon
5 cups water
2 ½ T. cornstarch
2 T. lemon juice
Oil for frying
Powdered sugar for dusting

Prepare pastry by placing shortening and flour in large mixing bowl. Cut shortening into flour. In separate bowl, combine egg, water, salt and vinegar, while stirring together, pour into flour mixture and blend well. Pinch off small amount of dough and roll out on a floured board. Using extra large biscuit cutter, bowl, saucer or other implement as a guide, cut into a circle. Repeat until all dough has been cut. Put 1 tablespoon filling on each circle, fold pastry over to form a half circle. Seal by pressing a floured fork around the edge. Heat 1-2" of oil in skillet or frying pan. Place a few pies in hot oil and cook until they turn a golden brown on the bottom, turn over and fry other side. Drain on rack over paper towels. Dust with powdered sugar.

For Filling, in medium saucepan, cook apples in the water for about 20 minutes or until tender. In a bowl, combine sugar, cornstarch and cinnamon. Add to the apples, then add the lemon juice. Cook until mixture has thickened, the remove from heat. Cool mixture before filling pastry circles. Makes about 2 dozen.

Variation:
Add 1/3 cups raisins to the saucepan with the apples and increase the water to 5 ¼ cups. Stew fruit as directed above.

APRICOT FRIED PIES

9 ounce package dried apricot halves
1 ¼ cups water
½ cup sugar
½ tsp. cinnamon
½ tsp. nutmeg
1 T. fresh lemon or orange juice
Pie crust dough – see recipe above or use 1 15 oz. package refrigerated piecrusts
Oil for frying
Powdered sugar

In medium saucepan, combine apricots and 1 ¼ cups water and bring to a boil. Cover, reduce heat and simmer for 20 minutes or until fruit is tender. Using a fork, mash fruit. Stir in sugar, cinnamon and nutmeg. Set aside to cool while you prepare pastry circles.

Prepare pie crust and roll out to 1/8" thickness. Cut into 5 inch circles. Spoon 2 T. of cooled filling on each circle. Moisten edge with water, fold over and crimp edges with a fork. Pour 1-2" of oil into large heavy skillet. Fry pies in hot oil (375 degrees Fahrenheit), about 2 minutes or until golden brown on both sides. Drain well on paper towels. Sprinkle with powdered sugar. Makes about 10 pies Variation:

Substitute apricots with pitted prunes. Substitute nutmeg with 1 tsp. orange zest.

Proceed as directed above.

DRIED CHERRY FRIED PIES

Follow pastry ingredients for Apple Fried Pies and cut into 5 inch circles
6 ounce package dried cherries, chopped
1 cup water
½ cup sugar
½ tsp. almond extract
Oil for frying
2 cups sifted powdered sugar
½ cup milk
½ tsp. vanilla

In medium saucepan, combine cherries and water. Let sit for a half hour to allow the cherries to absorb water. Bring to a boil over medium heat, then reduce heat and simmer, stirring often, for 20 minutes or until liquid has evaporated. Allow filling to cool.

Place 2 T. filling on each circle, moisten edge with water and crimp with fork. Heat 1-2" oil in heavy skillet to 375 degrees Fahrenheit. Fry pies, a few at a time, until golden brown on each side. Drain on paper towels.

Prepare glaze by adding milk to powdered sugar and stirring rapidly until it is smooth. Add the vanilla. Spoon and spread over each pie, allow dry to rack before eating.

Variation:
When filling begins to cool, add ½ cup chopped almonds.

FRESH PEACH FRIED PIES

2 cups flour
1 tsp. baking powder
½ cup butter
6 T. cold water
2 cups fresh peeled and chopped peaches
1/3 cup sugar
4 T. water, divided
¼ tsp. cinnamon
1 T. cornstarch
Oil for frying
Sugar for sprinkling or finish with sugar glaze made with powdered sugar, milk and vanilla

In a medium bowl, combine 2 cups flour and 1 tsp. baking powder. Cut in butter. Blend until mixture is fine crumbs. Sprinkle with 6 T. cold water and blend with fork. Work with hands until pastry holds together. On floured board, roll out pastry to 1/8" thickness. Cut out 15 5" circles.

In large saucepan, combine peaches, sugar 2 T. water and cinnamon. Stirring occasionally, bring to a boil over medium heat. Boil for 2 minutes. In a bowl, combine the cornstarch and the remaining 2 T. water. Stir until smooth, then add to peaches. Stir constantly, bring to a boil and cook another minute. Pour into bowl, cover with plastic wrap and allow to cool.

Place 1 T. filling on each circle, moisten edge and crimp with a fork, pressing edge to avoid leakage. Heat oil in large heavy saucepan, filled with oil no more than a third. Heat to 375 degrees Fahrenheit. Carefully add pies, two at a time. Fry, turning once, 4 minutes or until golden. Drain on paper towels. If desired, sprinkle pies with sugar or cover in a thin sugar glaze.

DRIED PEACH FRIED PIES

1 cup dried peaches, chopped
¾ cup water
¼ cup sugar
½ tsp. almond extract
¼ tsp. cinnamon

Pastry, prepared as for Fresh Peach Fried Pies
Oil for frying
Sugar for dusting

Prepare pastry and cut into 5" rounds.

Combine dried peaches and water in a small saucepan. Let stand for 30 minutes. Bring peaches and water to a boil over medium heat, reduce heat, and cook while stirring often for at least 10 minutes. Fruit should be tender and liquid has evaporated. Remove from heat, add sugar, almond extract and cinnamon. Stir until sugar dissolves. Cool.

When filling is cool, place 2 T. filling on each pastry circle, moisten edge, fold over and press down. Crimp edge with fork. Heat 1-2" of oil in heavy large skillet to 375 degrees Fahrenheit. Fry a few at time until golden brown on both sides. Drain on paper towels. Dust with sugar.

PINEAPPLE HAND PIES

2/3 cup chopped dried pineapple
½ cup pineapple juice
¼ cup water
1/3 cup sugar
Pastry prepared into 5" circles
Oil for frying

Combine pineapple, juice and water in a small saucepan, let stand 1 hour. Bring mixture to a boil over medium heat, then reduce heat, and cook, stirring often, 15 minutes or until pineapple is tender and liquid has evaporated. Remove from heat and add sugar. Stir until sugar dissolves. Cool.

Place 2 T. filling on each pastry circle. Moisten edge and fold over. Press together, then crimp with a fork. Heat 1-2" oil in a heavy large skillet to 375 degrees Fahrenheit. Fry a few pies at a time until golden brown. Drain on paper towels.

OLD TIMEY RAISIN PIES

1 large box of raisins
¼ cup flour
½ cup sugar
Standard pie crust for 2 double crust pies
Oil for frying
Powdered sugar for dusting

Place raisins in large saucepan and cover with water so that there is 1 inch over the raisins. Over medium heat, bring the mixture to a boil and let cook for 15 minutes. Meanwhile, mix the flour and sugar together in a small bowl. When raisins have finished cooking, remove saucepan from heat and stir in the flour-sugar mixture. Raisins should have a good consistency for spreading. If too soupy, chill in refrigerator for a short time until it thickens up.

Roll out pie crust and cut into 5" diameter circles. Place 1 tablespoon of raisin mixture on each circle, fold over and crimp edges with a fork. Heat oil to 375 degrees Fahrenheit. When oil reaches temperature, fry a few at a time until golden brown on both sides and drain on brown paper. Dust with powdered sugar.

Variation:
Add zest of 1 lemon or 1 orange to filling when you add the flour-sugar mixture. Stir well to blend.

When pies have been filled and crimped, prick tops with a fork. Brush with melted butter and sprinkle cinnamon sugar on top. Place on ungreased cookie sheet and bake in a preheated oven at 375 degrees Fahrenheit.

LOUISIANA STYLE MEAT PIES

1 pound each of ground beef and ground pork
1 medium yellow onion, chopped
1 medium green bell pepper, chopped
1 bunch of green onions, chopped
4-5 garlic cloves, minced
1 T. flour
1 tsp. salt
½ tsp freshly ground black pepper
½ tsp. cayenne pepper
3 dashes Tabasco sauce
8 cups flour
2 tsp. baking powder
1 tsp. salt
1 cup shortening
2 eggs, beaten
2 ¼ cups milk

Combine meat in a heavy large skillet and brown over medium heat, stirring so that it crumbles. Remove meat from skillet to drain, leaving fat in the skillet. Add the onions, bell pepper, green onion and garlic. Cook and stir until vegetables are soft and tender. Return meat to skillet and blend with the vegetables. Add flour, salt, black pepper, cayenne pepper and Tabasco to the meat mixture and stir through. Set aside to cool.

Combine flour, baking powder and salt in a large bowl. Cut in the shortening with a pastry blender until mixture resembles course meal. Combine eggs and milk and gradually add to flour mixture with a fork. Stir until all dry ingredients are moistened. Shape into a ball. Pastry will be stiff. Divide ball into 4 portions. Roll out 1 portion at a time to 1/8" thick on a floured board. Cut 5 6" circles from each portion of pastry.

Spoon ¼ cup of meat mixture on each circle. Moisten edge and fold over, pressing down. Crimp edge with a fork. Pour 2" of oil in a large skillet to 375 degrees Fahrenheit. Fry a few pies at a time until browned on both sides. Drain on paper towels. Serve immediately.

SWEETIE

This reporter has arrived at the McCoy residence on Weaver Road. The blue ranch-style house is well maintained. The front yard groomed and sports five blue spruce trees stair-stepping in height, representing each of the McCoy children. The front door pops open and Peggy Sue McCoy waves me in.

"Come on in, the pies are still coolin' off," Peggy Sue says. "Do you have a few minutes? I'll give you the recipes in the meantime."

Peggy Sue just turned thirty but she still maintains her girlish figure appearing to be a teenager, half her age. It's hard to believe that she is the church secretary, mother of five, substitute teacher, little league coach, part-time ballet teacher. Where does she get the energy? She's been married for twelve years, still in love with her high school sweetheart, Tommy, She often wears his flannel shirts over a light tee shirt with her jeans.

"I don't go a day without wearing one of Tommy's shirts. I just love him so much. I can smell his scent on his shirts even though they're laundered. So he's with me all day long while he's at work. I know that sounds crazy but I can't stop myself!" She smiled.

"What can you tell me about your pies today? Is there any special story about your recipes?"'

"Yes, actually, there is. I've been able to work through the depression and stuff. I can talk about it now. Thank you, Jesus! I remember that it was a chilly winter day. The house was cold. In those days, Tommy and I had a hard time financially. We had to budget everything to keep things going. I didn't want to turn on the heat. I didn't think we could afford it. I had put these little sweat pant outfits on the kids over their regular clothes to keep them warm. Since I had to do the laundry, I thought it would be a good time to. I liked to fold clothes right out of the dryer to keep warm. I was sitting on the sofa folding clothes and putting them in piles for each of the kid's rooms. I remember Matthew sitting on the floor in front of the TV watching cartoons. Mark and Luke were sitting across from each other at the coffee table. They were halfway watching television and halfway playing a game. The baby, Sarah, was rocking in her swing.

"Suddenly, I realized that Mark and Luke were fighting. Mark was pinching Luke and Luke was punching him back. They were yelling and screaming at each other. Sarah was crying hysterically in her swing. Matthew just sat there ignoring it all. I was watching this all happen and yet I was frozen. Totally incapable of doing anything. I was crying on the inside yet nobody could hear me or help me. I remember moving to my side and lying on the sofa, sort of moving into a ball. Help me! Help me! I cried. Then I asked the Lord to help me. I told him that I was tired. I fell asleep. I don't know how long I was out. I remember asking the Lord in my dream to help me get some rest. When I woke up, everything was wonderful. Matthew was playing with Sarah in her swing and she was giggling so happily. Such a joy she was. Mark and Luke were sitting quietly watching their favorite show. The house was warm. I thought I had received a message something about paradise just before I woke up. It all seemed like a dream. I sat up and asked the kids if they wanted to help me make a pie. I picked up Sarah and put her in her high chair. The boys followed me into the kitchen. I gave Sarah a graham cracker to munch and the boys crunched the rest in a bowl for the crust. They were so good and helpful. I took a jar of tropical fruit juice out of the pantry and cooked a filling. It was hard to believe that anything had happened. I devised the pie and it was the best we ever tasted. The pie looked like a tropical sunset, it was the most beautiful color I had ever seen.

"When Tommy came home from work that night he reported that he had been promoted to supervisor. Things looked up from then on. Every time we need something special, I always make my paradise pie."

"Wow! That's quite a tale, Peggy Sue."

"Yeah, I know. I can't explain all of it. I think I was kind of stressed out then. You know, we married young. I wanted to be a teacher and started college. My mother got sick and I had to quit school to nurse her. She died of the cancer six months later. My daddy was killed shortly thereafter in a tractor accident. I had six pregnancies in 5 years. Lost one. When everything is said and done, I'm one lucky woman. We went through a lot. I've learned that we can face and overcome anything that life throws at us. The key is to keep your home filled with love and hope now. Maybe my paradise pie will help someone else too."

PEGGY SUE'S PARADISE PIE

1 prepared baked pie shell
½ cup cornstarch
4 ½ cups tropical fruit juice, such as guava, passionfruit, pineapple or combination
1 T. fresh lemon juice
Meringue or whipped cream for topping

Garnish with canned apricot halves and toasted sliced almonds, sliced bananas and flaked coconut or crushed pineapple.

Prepare and bake pie shell. Set aside to cool. In a cup, mix cornstarch and ½ cup of the fruit juice, whisk together until smooth, then set aside.

In a medium saucepan, stir the sugar into the remaining fruit juice and bring to a boil. Continue stirring to make sure that the sugar has dissolved. When at a full rolling boil, reduce heat and stir in the cornstarch mixture. Allow filling to simmer, stirring occasionally. Cook for about 5 minutes or until mixture thickens and coats the back of a spoon. Remove from heat and blend in lemon juice. Allow mixture to cool for 30 minutes, then pour into prepared pie shell. If using meringue as a topping, prepare meringue and spread over the pie filling. Place in a moderately hot oven for 3-5 minutes until the meringue peaks have turned lightly brown, then remove from oven. Place in refrigerator to chill for at least 2 hours before serving.

If serving with whipped cream, pipe along edge of crust. Top with apricot halves and sprinkle with almonds, sliced bananas and flaked coconut or spoon crushed pineapple over the whipped cream.

MOM'S STRAWBERRY FLUFF PIE

1 prepared pie shell, baked at 300 degrees Fahrenheit for 45 minutes, then cool
1 small package strawberry jello, made with only 1 cup boiling water
6 egg whites, divided
1 cup sugar, divided
¼ tsp. cream of tartar
Pinch of salt
¼ cup ripe strawberries forced through a sieve
½ cup water
Prepare strawberry jello and chill in the refrigerator.

Take 4 egg whites and beat until stiff with the cream of tartar and ¾ cup of the sugar. Beat the chilled jello into the egg whites and return to the refrigerator.

In a small saucepan, place the sieved strawberries, ½ cup water and the remaining ¼ cup of sugar. Cook over medium heat for 15 minutes, stirring constantly. Remove from heat and allow cool slightly.

Whip the remaining 2 egg whites with a pinch of salt until stiff, then add the strawberry mixture. Remove jello from refrigerator and whip the jello. Fold in the strawberry mixture, blending well. Pour into prepared pie shell. Chill for at least 4 hours to set before serving.

GRANDMA FRY'S FAVORITE CHIFFON PIE

1 package unflavored gelatin
½ cup sugar
Pinch of salt

1 box red ripe strawberries, divided
½ cup water
3 eggs, separated
½ cup heavy cream, whipped

1 prepared pie shell, baked, graham cracker or cookie crumb crust

Take two-thirds of the strawberries, trim tops and place in a blender. Reserve remaining strawberries for garnish. Puree strawberries and pour into a bowl. In a saucepan, combine the gelatin with the sugar and salt, then add the water. Over a medium heat, stir until mixture almost comes to a boil, then remove from heat. Add strawberry puree.

Lightly beat the egg yolks, then stir a small amount of hot gelatin strawberry mixture into them to temper. Then stir egg yolk mixture into the saucepan with hot gelatin strawberry mixture. Over low heat, cook mixture for one minute, stirring constantly. Remove from heat and place in refrigerator. Chill until mixture thickens. It should mound when dropped from a spoon.

Beat egg whites until stiff, then fold in the gelatin mixture and the beaten whipped cream, until thoroughly blended. Pour into prepared pie crust and chill until set, at least 3 hours.

Variation:

Coconut Chiffon – reduce water to ¼ cup. Sprinkle gelatin over water in a small bowl and let sit for 5 minutes. When egg yolks, sugar and salt are in the saucepan, add 1 ½ cups coconut milk. After cooking egg yolk mixture, stir in softened gelatin and chill as directed. Fold ¾ cup shredded coconut and 1 tsp. vanilla into egg yolk mixture, proceed again as directed. Garnish with toasted coconut.

Light Lemon Chiffon – increase sugar to 1 cup, water to 2/3 cup and increase eggs to 4. Delete whipped cream from recipe. In a saucepan, combine the gelatin, ½ of the sugar, water and egg yolks, stir until blended. Cook, stirring over low heat until mixture just thickens, about 10-15 minutes. Stir in 1/3 cup lemon juice and 1 T. grated fresh lemon zest. Remove from heat and chill. Beat egg whites with ½ tsp. cream of tartar and remaining sugar, blend with lemon mixture, fold into pie crust and chill.

Lime Chiffon – substitute strawberries for 1/3 cup fresh lime juice and 1 T. grated lime zest. Increase water to 2/3 cups. Add the lime juice and zest to the gelatin sugar and salt, then heat as directed. Enhance color with a few drops green food coloring when combining the egg whites with gelatin mixture and whipped cream, if desired. Garnish pie with a thinly sliced lime.

Mandarin Orange Chiffon – Eggs are deleted from the recipe. Soften gelatin by sprinkling over 2 T. cold water. Stir in 1 cup of boiling water. Increase sugar to 1 cup. Stir sugar into the boiling water until sugar has dissolved. Add ½ cup fresh lemon juice. Refrigerate mixture until thickened but not set. Whip cream until thick and fold into the gelatin mixture, then add 1 11 oz. can of drained mandarin oranges. Pour into baked pie shell and chill at least 4 hours before serving. Garnish with additional mandarin orange slices on top.

Orange Chiffon–Substitute water for ½ cup fresh orange juice. Combine gelatin and orange juice, then set aside. Beat egg yolks with the sugar until well blended and slowly add ¾ cup scalded milk, slightly cooled, stirring constantly. Cook over low heat until slightly thickened. Remove from heat, stir in 1 tsp. grated fresh orange zest and the gelatin mixture. Proceed as directed above.

Pumpkin Chiffon – Reduce water to ¼ cup. Sprinkle gelatin over the water and set aside. In a medium saucepan, add the egg yolks and beat until frothy. Add 1 cup canned pumpkin 1/3 cup of the sugar, the pinch of salt, ½ tsp. cinnamon, ½ tsp. allspice, ¼ tsp. ground ginger, ¼ tsp. ground nutmeg, ½ cup milk. Cook over medium heat until mixture begins to thicken, about 10 minutes. Stir in gelatin mixture and allow mixture to cool. Beat the egg whites with the remaining sugar and proceed as directed above.

Raspberry Chiffon – Substitute strawberries with raspberries. Rather than placing raspberries in a blender, place in a medium bowl, 1 pint of fresh raspberries and crush them with a fork or potato masher. Add ¼ cup of sugar to the berries and let sit for 30 minutes. Push raspberries through a sieve to remove the seeds. Discard seeds. Add the raspberry pulp plus 1 T. fresh lemon juice to the gelatin mixture and proceed as directed. Garnish with additional raspberries, if desired.

Red Grapefruit Chiffon – increase sugar to ¾ cup. To the gelatin, sugar and salt, add 1 ½ cups fresh red grapefruit juice and 2 tsp. grated fresh red grapefruit zest. After adding egg yolk mixture to the gelatin, add 2 T. fresh lemon juice and chill as directed.

Tangerine Chiffon – Follow directions for the red grapefruit but substitute the juice and zest from thin skinned tangerines instead. Garnish pie with a tangerine, peeled and sectioned.

Watermelon Chiffon – Use 3 egg whites only. Start with about 3 ½ pounds ripe watermelon. Discard rind and seeds. Cut melon into cubes and whirl in a blender. Pour through a strainer, discard pulp, measure out 1 ½ cups juice. Place juice into a saucepan, stir in 1/3 cup sugar and salt. Sprinkle gelatin on top and let stand for 5 minutes. Over medium heat, stir until gelatin and sugar dissolves., then stir in 2 tsp. fresh lemon juice. Chill. Proceed as directed above.

BLACK-BOTTOM PIE

1/3 cup sugar
4 tsp. cornstarch
2 cups half and half
6 egg yolks
3 oz. semi-sweet chocolate, finely chopped
2 oz. unsweetened chocolate, finely chopped
1 packet unflavored gelatin
2 T. cold water
2 T. dark rum
4 egg whites Pinch of salt
¼ cup sugar
1 cup heavy cream, whipped
1 9" prepared chocolate pastry shell
Chocolate shavings for garnish

Mix the 1/3 cup sugar and cornstarch together in a medium saucepan. Over medium heat, gradually stir in the half and half. Cook for about 10 minutes. Mixture will thicken to the consistency of heavy cream. Remove from heat.

In a medium mixing bowl, beat egg yolks until the yolks ribbon slightly when the beater is lifted. Then, whisk in about half of the half and half mixture, blend, then pour everything into the half and half mixture still in the saucepan. Cook, stirring constantly, over medium heat until it thickens to the consistency of pudding. Strain 1 1/3 cups of the hot custard into a small bowl, adding the chopped chocolates and stirring until it has melted. Reserve the remaining custard.

Sprinkle the gelatin over 2 T. cold water in a small bowl. Let stand a couple of minutes, until the gelatin has softened. Place bowl over a pan of hot water and stir until the gelatin has melted. Stir the gelatin into the plain the custard. Whisk in the rum. Strain mixture into a large bowl. Refrigerate, stirring about every 3 minutes, until cold but not set, about 10 minutes altogether.

Spread chocolate custard in the bottom of the chocolate pastry shell, cover loosely and refrigerate.

Beat egg whites and salt in a large mixing bowl at medium speed until soft peaks form. Beat in the ¼ cup sugar, a spoonful at a time, until peaks are stiff and glossy. Fold egg whites into the cold custard. Fold in a ½ cup of the whipped cream. Refrigerate 5 minutes to thicken slightly, then pour into pie shell over the chocolate layer. Mound custard slightly in the center. Refrigerate for 5 minutes until filling has set slightly. Spread remaining whipped cream over the pie, sprinkle top with chocolate shavings. Chill at least 4 hours before serving.

BRANDY ALEXANDER PIE

1 9" graham cracker crust pie shell
1 cup sugar
6 eggs, beaten
1 packet unflavored gelatin
½ cup water
2 cups whipping cream
1 T. crème de cacao
1 T. brandy, use best quality
¾ cup semi-sweet chocolate, shaved

Gradually add sugar to beaten eggs, constantly beating, until fluffy. In a small saucepan, sprinkle gelatin into ½ cup water, then stir and dissolve gelatin. Over medium high heat, bring gelatin and water to a boil. While beating, slowly add hot gelatin mixture into eggs. When thoroughly blended, set aside to cool. Chill in refrigerator until thickened but not yet set.

Whip cream until stiff but not dry, then gently fold into cooled egg mixture. Add crème de cacao and brandy. Spoon into prepared pie shell. Sprinkle with chocolate shavings. Chill for at least 4 hours before serving.

CHOCOLATE-ORANGE TRUFFLE PIE

1 packet unflavored gelatin
1/3 cup fresh orange juice
1 6 oz. pkg. semi-sweet chocolate chips
1 tsp. vanilla
1 tsp. grated orange zest
2 eggs, separated
¼ cup sugar
1 ½ cups heavy cream, whipped
1 8" prepared chocolate crumb pie crust

In a medium saucepan, sprinkle gelatin over the fresh orange juice and let sit for 5 minutes. Over a low heat, stir gelatin mixture until gelatin has dissolved. Add chocolate chips and continue stirring until the chocolate has melted. Remove from heat, add vanilla and orange zest, blending in well. Let cool for about 10 minutes.

While gelatin mixture is cooling, in a large mixing bowl, beat eggs with sugar on high speed until thickened, about 7-8 minutes. Gradually add the gelatin mixture and beat until just blended. Fold in the whipped cream. Turn into prepared pie shell and chill four 4 hours before serving. Garnish with additional whipped cream and chocolate shavings.

Variation:
Mocha – substitute the orange juice with freshly brewed but cold coffee. Substitute orange zest with 1 T. instant coffee or espresso granules. Add coffee granules with the chocolate chips.

GRASSHOPPER PIE

1 packet unflavored gelatin
1 ¼ cups heavy cream
¼ cup sugar
¼ cup green crème de menthe
¼ cup white crème de cacao
4 large egg yolks
1 9" prepared chocolate crumb crust
Chocolate shavings for garnish

In a medium stainless steel mixing bowl, sprinkle the gelatin over ¼ cup of the heavy cream. Let it soften for 5 minutes. Whisk in the sugar, the liqueurs, and the egg yolks. Set the bowl over a saucepan of simmering hot water, stirring constantly. Cook until mixture reaches 160 degrees Fahrenheit on a candy thermometer. Transfer bowl to sit in a larger bowl of ice and chilled water. Continue to stir until the mixture has cooled and thickened.

In a separate bowl, beat the remaining cup of heavy cream until stiff. Fold it into the crème de menthe mixture. Pour filling into prepared pie shell and chill for 4 hours before serving. Sprinkle with shaved chocolate to serve.

Variation:
Substitute unflavored gelatin mixture by melting 4 cups of miniature marshmallows in ½ cup milk. Delete the sugar and egg yolks. When completely melted, let cool slightly, then blend in the liqueurs. Let mixture cool completely. Increase the whipped cream to 2 cups total. Blend 1 ½ cups whipped cream into the crème de menthe mixture and pour into the pie shell. Reserve the remaining ½ cup whipped cream for garnish.

MARGARITA PIE

1 packet unflavored gelatin
1 cup sugar
½ tsp salt
4 eggs, separated
1 cup fresh lime juice

1/3 cup tequila
2 T. triple sec liqueur
2 tsp. grated lime zest
1 baked 9" pie shell

Combine gelatin, ½ cup sugar and salt in medium saucepan. In small mixing bowl, beat egg yolks. Add lime juice and continue beating until frothy. Add egg yolks to gelatin mixture. Cook over low heat for 3-5 minutes until gelatin is dissolved. Remove from heat and stir in tequila, triple sec and lime zest. Chill mixture until mixture is thick but not quite set.

Beat egg whites until foamy, then gradually add the sugar, continuing to beat until egg whites are stiff. Fold egg whites into gelatin mixture. Spoon into pie crust and chill for 4 hours before serving. Garnish with lime twists.

Variation:
For strawberry margarita, hull and slice 2 cups of red ripe strawberries, sprinkle with ¼ cup of sugar. Set aside. Add to the gelatin and egg yolk mixture, then cook as directed above.

MAI TAI PIE

1 packet unflavored gelatin
¼ cup sugar
4 eggs, separated
1 6 oz. can unsweetened pineapple juice
¼ cup fresh lime juice
1/3 cup rum
2 T. triple sec liqueur
¼ cup sugar
½ cup heavy cream, whipped
1 9" prepared pie shell

In a small saucepan, mix gelatin and ¼ cup sugar together. Beat in egg yolks until well blended, then gradually add pineapple juice. Turn onto medium heat and cook mixture until slightly thickened. Mixture should not boil. Remove from heat and stir in lime juice, rum, and liqueur. Pour into large bowl and place in freezer to chill down. Stir occasionally to assure that mixture is thickening up.

While gelatin mixture chills, whip egg whites in a medium mixing bowl until foamy, then gradually add remaining ¼ cup sugar. Beat until meringue is stiff. Fold into gelatin mixture with the whipped cream. Spoon into prepared pie shell.

GREEK STYLE HONEY PIE

1 9" prepared Greek style pastry crust
1 ½ lbs. cream cheese
¾ cup sugar
1 tsp. cinnamon + extra for sprinkling
1 tsp. fresh grated lemon zest
2 tsp. fresh lemon juice
1 cup honey
6 eggs
Powdered sugar for sprinkling

Preheat oven to 325 degrees Fahrenheit. In a large mixing bowl, beat the cream cheese with the sugar, 1 tsp. cinnamon, lemon zest and lemon juice until smooth. Blend in the honey, then add the eggs, one at a time. Mixture should be very creamy. Pour into the prepared pie shell. Bake at 325 degrees for 45 minutes, then increase temperature to 375 degrees and continue baking for 15 minutes or until light brown. Combine about ½ tsp cinnamon with 1 tsp powdered sugar. Using thumb and forefinger, sprinkle powdered sugar in lines across top of pie in a grid design.

12

WOW! PAGES AND PAGES OF stories and recipes never ending. Ruta Mae has done a fantastic job. Well, maybe some of these "biographies" are a little too personal, a little too graphic, heart-warming and tragic, but the girl sure knows how to reel in the reader with her writing. Oh my gosh, it was 6 AM and I needed to get ready for the big day. I don't have time to continue reading. That will have to wait until some night when I can lounge in the bathtub and relax.

Oh Charley, I wish you were here, you big lug. This would be your day. I'm so sorry you will miss it. I hope you'll watch over us and enjoy yourself.

Pamela and I spent all early morning baking and stocking shelves, putting out extra inventory. Pamela surprised me with additional items she placed in baskets, miniature pie tins, cookie cutters and baking accoutrements she thought would sell especially this day during the contest. The square looked particularly pretty. Overnight, the square had been decorated with bunting and banners and I suddenly noticed that the television news team had shown up. I stepped outside to get a better look at the activities when I saw the white Cadillac convertible approach on the highway. As it came close, I waved and sure enough James Beard was driving with Julia in the front seat just as I pictured. They pulled in front of the store and parked. I guess I was so excited I didn't even notice at first the tour bus pull in behind it.

"James! Julia!" I screamed. "Oh, Minnie Pearl!, Roy!"

They all exited their vehicles simultaneously and we had a group hug standing there in the sidewalk.

"Come in, ya'll! Welcome to Silent Springs, Arkansas. Pamela, meet our royal guests!" I yelled as I opened the door and ushered everyone into the store. Another group hug ensued inside the store.

"Francine, I am so sorry, honey. We're here for you and Charley." James Beard said. "Oh my, who is this lovely creature?"

"This is Pamela. She's been a tremendous help to me since I lost Charley. Let us show you around the store a bit. Care for some coffee and pastries or a nice cup of tea?" I asked.

"Yes, please!" Julia responded. "Oh my! Jim! Jim? We left Irma out in the car!"

"Let me round up the refreshments," Pamela offered.

"I'll go out and get her." James said, his big smile flashing teeth. As he walked out the sun blinded us when it hit his bald head and flashed into our eyes.

"We picked Irma up in Hot Springs. She was there at the big hotel recuperating, taking the waters, so to speak. Taking a break from her strenuous schedule, she told us. Jim and I decided to pick her up while on our road trip. We had some great barbeque last night, spent the night there ourselves. Wonderful place, ever been?" Julia asked. "Anyway, as we were getting ready to leave this morning, she was stung by a bee. She started getting all puffy and loopy. Jim and I had to take her to the emergency room. They gave her a shot and it seemed to knock her out. She slept all the way here. I worried about her all the way here. Jim said she would be fine, just needed to sleep it off."

James escorted Irma inside and led her to a table where he seated her gently. Minnie Pearl sat down next to her and patted her arm.

"I am sorry, everyone." Irma apologized as she smoothed her hair down and away from her face. "Once I get some strong coffee in me, I'll be good to go. I never realized I was allergic to bees, until today." She giggled.

Pamela served coffee to everyone while I called Lou Evans and let him know I was holding the judges captive and safe from the public. I locked the door and flipped the sign showing I was closed. I can reopen once the judges go to work.

"Mam, I'm sorry 'bout your husband and all." Roy Clark offered. "Great place you have here! I'll do my very best to entertain while this guy and gals do all the hard work. I hope ya'll are hungry 'cuz we're here in the South and Southern cooks sure know how to make good pies!"

"Roy, are you saying you can't get a good piece of apple pie in New York City? Let me tell you right now, I know a great place!" James responded.

"No offense, sir, but this is the South. Nothin' like it!" Roy Clark smiled.

"Well, son, what about Washington State or Minnesota? They both grow fantastic apples. Surely, you can find excellent pies elsewhere. This is America." James responded. "You can find pie everywhere."

"Yeah, well just wait. Like I said before, this is the South. This is a whole new ball game. These folks are goin' ta' bust your chops!" Roy went on.

"You choosing me off? Are you picking a fight with me, country boy? Banjo picker?" James now said, getting red in the face. "Sarah, maybe it wasn't a good idea bringing him with you." He looked at Minnie Pearl meekly.

"Now, now, boys! Simmer down." Minnie Pearl said. She reached over and threw her arm over Roy's chest. "Jimmy, I think Roy is a just givin' you fair warning this is not goin' ta' be a cake walk. Roy's done plenty of country fairs and let me tell you, it's not easy."

"That's right," Julia said. "It's not a cake walk, it's a pie contest, you silly goose! Sit down, Jimmy, and have your coffee."

James Beard pulled out a chair and sat down at the table between Roy and myself. I patted his arm. He smiled and everyone recognized he had been trying to create a little drama. I thought he had done it to lighten the atmosphere. No one likes to attend a funeral. Hard to be here with Charley gone.

"This is really difficult for me to verbalize," I started to say, "but I want to thank all of you for coming and helping me. I am so sad that Charley is not here to enjoy your company. It's been really difficult. I am so honored." My eyes were kind of tearing up and my throat was starting to choke.

"Now, now." They said in unison. "We want to be here and we want to honor Charley and his memory. He was a great chef, a great friend, a great husband." Julia spoke.

"To Charley!" Pamela said as she raised her coffee cup to James Beard's and clinked his cup. Everyone toasted Charley and we took a sip.

"I like this gal," James said. "Reminds me of my mother." He winked at Pamela. "She was British, you know."

Pamela was beaming. Her blue eyes twinkled with excitement.

Lou Evans walked up to the front door and knocked. Pamela let him in and relocked the door. Another round of introductions took place and then Lou provided all the instructions as to how everything was scheduled.

"Irma, how are you feeling?" I asked. "If you don't think you are feeling well enough, you don't have to do this. I didn't ask but do you need some ice on your sting?"

"I'm fine now, absolutely fine. A little itchy, maybe, but it will go away.

Nothing would stop me except a new bee sting. I'm ready."

"OK, but if you start feeling sick or not too well, please let us know. You will, won't you?"

"Of course! Don't worry about me. Let's go!"

[13]

WE WERE ABOUT READY TO leave the shop and move to the stage area on the square when I saw Lucky walking towards the highway ready to cross with something huge.

"Pamela, look at that! Look! It's Lucky." I said "What's she carrying?"

"My stars, Francine! That woman is just dreadful." Pamela answered.

James Beard looked to the left to see what we were talking about and he had a strange look on his face. Everyone left the store and I turned to lock the door. We walked in a group. James and Julia each flanking my sides. Lou was leading us.

The next thing I know, Lou was introducing the crowd to our guest judges when suddenly Lucky appeared from the crowd holding the biggest pie I have ever seen in my life and stood in front of the stage. Her arms outstretched cradling a pie three feet in diameter.

Lou was standing with the microphone when he saw her standing there and was suddenly speechless. James looked down at the woman again with that strange look on his face.

"Four and twenty blackbirds baked in a pie, please tell me where to take this lest my arms fall off and die!" Lucky cried.

"Dear me!" Lou said. "Mam, let me help you with that. Folks, let me get that last entry onto the cart for this poor woman." He handed the microphone to Minnie Pearl.

"Howdeeee! I'm jest so proud to be here!" Minnie Pearl smiled and pinched her dress out, flaring the skirt slightly. The tag on her hat flipped back and forth flashing $1.98 every second.

The crowd yelled back, "Howdeee!" The cheers were deafening.

THE PRICKLEBERRY PIE CONTEST

"I'm so happy to be here in Silent Springs, Arkansas for the Prickleberry Pie Contest! I gotta tell ya' it is BEE-YOU-TI-FULL here! You should be so proud of your fine town. Now, yesta'day me and Roy left Grinder's Switch. My stomach's a grumblin' for somethin' good to eat. I couldn't wait to get here. Ah'm so hungry! The corn's not in yet and Uncle Nabob is still feeding and fattenin' the pig. I tole Brother that I'd bring him a slice o'pie when I come home. Well folks, I got me a job to do, and I'll be back on stage with the winners. In the meantime, enjoy yourself and please pay special attention to my good friend, Roy Clark! I love you so much it hurts!"

With that said, Minnie Pearl handed the microphone to Roy and stepped off the stage with James, Julia, Irma and Lou. The crowd clapped and cheered. Pamela and I walked to the Chuckwagon Café with everyone. Lou and Kathy had done an excellent job in setting up the judging table. The area outside the window where the four of them would sit and taste test was roped off. The tables were spread with hundreds of pies and I mean hundreds. The café was split in two. They were trying to maintain business in the half nearest the kitchen and the remaining half was filled with pies of every kind and flavor.

The judges walked around the room looking at the pies before they took their seats at the judging table. Kathy would provide the pies in batches by categories and whisk away the remainders.

"Sacré bleu! Est fantastique, eh, Jimmy?" Julia looked amazed.

"Crikey, there are more pies than lights on Broadway! I don't know if we can sample this many, Jules! This might be impossible," James said.

"This is what Roy was trying to warn you about. These folks take pie seriously." Minnie Pearl added. "I hate to say it," she whispered, "but I don't know if we can taste this many. What do ya'll think?"

Irma said, "You're right. I think we need to set some ground rules here before we get started. Honestly, we have to try every pie, but I don't think we can afford to take more than a small bite. I think we need to look, taste and quickly judge. This thing is going to take a long time." "Irma's right." Julia said.

Kathy brought them the pens, pencils and judging sheets. "Now, ya'll see there are a lot of categories and there are several factors in judging each sample.

Charley came up with all of it."

"He would." James said with a sly smile.

"Anyway, once you taste test each batch, I will remove the pie from the table. There will be no second tasting. We have too many pies to go through. Also, once the pies are removed, they will be taken outside. I'm sorry about that but that's the way it will have to be. The people will have the opportunity to taste and vote for 'The People's Choice' award. Ya'll have to be confident with your voting as is. I'll get you each a glass of ice water and some coffee and bring the refills. Is there anything else ya'll need? If there is anything else you think you need, please holler for me, OK? You will probably need some bathroom breaks so I recommend that you all break at the same time. You should probably do it at the end of a category. Anything else?"

All four of the judges shook their heads in agreement.

"My heavens, did you get a look at the score sheets? I'll never get home to Ohio!" Irma shook her head "This is crazy!"

"Are we ready?" James asked and everyone now shook their heads in the affirmative. "Alright, proprietor, bring it on!" "Let the games begin!" Julia perked up.

The judges looked out the window listening to Roy Clark and his banjo. The crowd filled the square and some of the contestants stood at the rope watching the judges just like they were looking at monkeys in the zoo. Kathy brought the first four pies to the table and they overheard someone yell "They've started the judging!" from the sidewalk.

In the meantime, Pamela and I made our way back to the shop and unlocked the door. We were followed in by at least two dozen customers hungry and thirsty for treats. This was going to be a record sales day, no question about it.

Two hours into the judging, Pamela and I finally had a slow down on our business. We could take a break. I could only imagine the activity at the judging table. With as many pies as I saw, I would not want to test them. My stomach would be declaring a revolution.

Pamela and I leaned against the counter to catch our breath. Then we both asked each other whether we should restock the shelves, the soda cooler, bake more cookies, make and pre-wrap some sandwiches. It was nearly noon. The lunch crowd would appear any second.

"Francine dear, can I ask you a question?"

"Sure, fire away!"

"Why did James Beard call Minnie Pearl, Sarah? Do you know? I didn't know who he was talking to, at first."

"Minnie Pearl's real name is Sarah. It is Sarah Ophelia Colley. That's her real name."

"Why? Is Minnie Pearl her nickname?"

"No, it's her stage name. People in show business use stage names."

"Oh. Why?"

"Why? There are number of reasons. Some people like the anonymity. Some people don't like their real name. When they get famous, they want some thing flashy, or romantic. Sometimes the movie studios will tell somebody they have to change their name. I can't explain it all but that's the way it is. Authors too. Some writers use pen names instead of their own. It all depends.

"Like who else?"

"Like a lot of movie stars and stuff. Take John Wayne for example. Do you know his real name is Marion?"

"No. Marion? Really? Marion?"

"Yes, Marion. Now, would you think he would be the strong type in the movies, if his name is Marion? Would you think him romantic, pillar of strength, adventurous, leading man, if his name was Marion?"

"No, I would think him to be a sissy. I remember a Marion in school. He was just a bookworm. He didn't play with the other boys at all."

"See my point? Minnie Pearl is more than a countrified bumpkin that sings country music and is a comedian. That is all an act. She is Sarah Ophelia Colley, a lady of means and education, arts, culture, leader in society and charities, loving wife. You'd never know that because all you see is her act."

"Thank you, Francine. My, I think I have been living in the country too long!"

"No, honey, as they say "That's show business!"

[14]

ILLUSIONS. WHILE PAMELA WAS AWAKENED to reality, it was hard for me to live it. All day in the back of my mind, I've thought about Charley every spare moment. It was even more difficult seeing James, Julia, Minnie Pearl and Irma here. All friends of Charley's and putting up a good show for their lost comrade. Listening to Lou on his microphone emceeing the day's proceedings from the stage hurt. I should have been listening to Charley's rich voice. Picturing him here today, seeing his presence, standing next to him, relishing on the huge turnout, the copious amounts of money coming into our town's coffers, seeing his exuberance and excitement with a successful endeavor. I admit I feel blue, depressed. It will probably be worse tomorrow when all the activity is over and the square looks like the world series was held in it. Then the responsibility will shift again to me, for a memorial service. I hope Lou doesn't get all misty eyed later on when the winners are announced and go into a history of how this all came about. Yes, illusions. I'll have to pretend that I'm OK and everything is fine. Even Pamela can't help me with that.

About the time I was nearly through my mental pity party, a young man entered the shop. I thought I'd seen him in here a few times.

"Oh, hello again!" I heard Pamela tell him. "Enjoying yourself with all the festivities over there?"

"Yes, it's been fun. The pie eating contest was really funny. That skinny girl nearly vacuumed her pie down before that tub o'lard wolfed down his pie. He choked on a big chunk of banana and the coconut flakes that stuck out on his face looked like he had kitty whiskers. She won, of course. It was pretty funny. Although I was afraid that he might need a paramedic for a while." The young man turned and nodded to me when he saw me. "Oh hey, Mrs. Simpson."

"It's Simson. Hi!" Correcting him.

"Simson? Not Simpson with a P? Sorry. I thought it was Simpson. I apologize, mam."

"That's OK," I said with a put-on smile and looked at him sweetly.

His face suddenly gave off the most serious look. "I gotta go." He announced and started for the door.

"Dear, can I help you with something?" Pamela asked. Her voice yelled out, "Is your friend better?"

He ran out of the store as fast as he could and down the highway. Pamela and I looked at each other.

"What happened there? That was strange enough, wasn't it though?"

"He didn't steal something did he?"

"No, he never took his hands out of his pockets. Oh, well."

"Look, here comes Ruta Mae! Maybe she can fill us in with what's happening out there." I watched as she entered the store and leaned across the counter and gave me a hug.

"Can I come back there?" She asked.

I nodded. "How is it going out there? Any word from the judges? I wonder how many pies they've tasted."

Ruta started rattling off facts so fast, I had to ask her to slow down.

"First of all, fifteen hundred cookbooks have sold already. We have another thousand left but they are flying off the table as fast as we can ring them up. You remember Tim Clary from Peregrine Publishing? Well, he told me that they are printing more as we speak because the sales are so good. They will be delivered later this afternoon. And, Francine, he asked me out on a date. Can you believe it? Also, he told me that his boss at Peregrine said that I was extremely talented. If I wanted to write another book, they would publish it for half cost. They are sure that I could have a best seller. Anyway, the news crew bought one of the cookbooks and they were so pleased with what I wrote, they asked me to come to the television station for a job interview. They think I have the skills to be a reporter or a journalist. Isn't that great?"

"Ruta Mae, I knew you were not only a beautiful girl, but extremely talented. I am so proud of you. You worked very hard on that cookbook and I am very grateful. You will be given a percentage of the profit, you know, for your hard work. Without you, it would not have happened. You said fifteen hundred cookbooks?"

"Yes, fifteen hundred already sold. Thank you, but I couldn't accept anything."

"Yes, you will and yes, you are! You deserve being paid for your hard work, Ruta Mae. Don't argue with me! Fifteen hundred…I can't get over it. Silent Springs only has a couple hundred people. Where did they all come from?"

"We have visitors from all over the county. OK, if you insist on paying me, I won't argue with you anymore. It has been a blast… Now listen to this, Lou Evans announced that there are four hundred and eighty pie entries! It's really going to take some time before they can decide on who will win. Little Sue Ellen Reynolds won the pie eating contest over Big Bill Barnes. She snorted down her pie and reported it was the best banana coconut cream pie she ever ate. Big Bill choked on a banana chunk making him lose the contest. I heard that Lou and Kathy Evan's dessert cook made chunky pies instead of just cream pies because Lou said the contestants always cheat by getting most of it on their faces anyways. He wanted to make sure that they had to eat them and not smear them around.

Then Tilly Ledbetter beat out Daisy Morgan at the pie balance and walk with holding twelve pies. Daisy only had ten but she dropped one. They had to walk twenty-five feet and also be the fastest one to reach the finish line.

I tell you what, Roy Clark is the best banjo player I ever seen! He is funny, he sings great and he sure can play!"

"Well, Ruta Mae, it sounds like you've had a really good time today so far!"

"Oh yes, mam! I gotta go now. I jes' wanted to tell you what was happening.

I'm going over to the window and see the celebrities. The news crew said James Beard nearly ate a whole pie by himself."

"Oh really?" Pamela asked. "What kind of pie was it?"

"I don't know but I can try and find out. See ya'll later!" Ruta jumped over the counter and sped out the door.

"Pamela?" Francine asked. "Pamela! Pamela, did you enter a pie?"

Pamela, looked at her square in the face with a sheepish grin. She turned and walked to the back of the shop, not answering.

We were stuck in the waiting game now. Four hundred and eighty pies! How long could it take four people to taste each one? This was going to be a long day. How long could Lou and Roy entertain the crowd? How long could Pamela and I stand being in the store? It was only a matter of time before our inventory was sold out. The clock started to tick ever so slowly. To kill time, I flipped through the finished cookbook that Ruta Mae had left.

PASTRY CRUSTS

Archie Redman was a nervous wreck. He had regrets about entering the pie contest. If his buddies knew he had entered the pie contest they would be ruthless in harassing him. Deep down, he wanted to win so bad but with a win, it would mean that he had subjected himself to merciless razzing. He knew he made a great pie and it should win, but Archie Redman was known as a tough man. He didn't need or want help ever from anyone. He didn't need a woman to cook, clean or keep him company. He didn't need anybody. He also made it clear to everyone that knew him that they better get any thoughts of domesticity right out of their heads or they'd be fixin' for a fight. He couldn't tell anyone that the secret of great pie crust was to keep the ingredients ice cold, work it as little as possible. Lard was better than butter or shortening to make it flaky. It tasted better too. The problem was that if he explained this to anyone, in his mind, they would think him a weakling. He wouldn't have it, couldn't stand it. There wasn't anything worse than being called a sissy.

Now, he was fighting remorse. He paced around the square hoping to win, hoping not to win, hoping to win. He stood outside the Chuckwagon Café, watched the judges in the window. Watched them look at each pie, taste each pie, make their marks on the score sheets. Was it his pie? Had they tasted it yet? Not tasted it yet? The suspense was killing him.

The afternoon heat was building and so were the clouds. This morning it had been a beautiful clear day. As the heat rose, the clouds grew. By noon, it was partly cloudy. They were still puffy and spread apart, moving quickly to east. Any good farmer could see that if they continued to build, we were in for a good gulley washer. Maybe, if we had a thunderstorm, everyone would go home. He would stay, of course, because he wanted to hear his name called and win the contest.

Maybe it was just the heat and humidity that was causing his intense perspiration and weak knees or maybe he needed some lunch. Yeah, that was it. He'd feel much better having a glass of ice cold sweet tea and a tuna salad sandwich. He entered the Chuckwagon Café and was directed to a seat. He sat down at his table staring at the judges the same way a hawk eyes a helpless chick.

15

"OH LORDY, I NEED A break!" Minnie Pearl said as she stretched in her seat. Just then she picked up her fork and rubbed boysenberry pie filling on her face. Irma looked at her. "What on God's green earth are you doing?"

"Ah'm goin' to take a break…Let me outta this here booth! And, give me that piece o' pie!" She said as she lifted the plate and an extra fork. "I'll be back in five."

"Minnie Pearl!" Julia reprimanded. "Come back here. You can't go out there with pie all over your face!"

"Just watch me!"

James Beard stood up and stretched, laughing in great big guffaws. "Look at that girl go! My, she makes me smile!"

Minnie Pearl moved swiftly through the crowd to the stage where Roy Clark had just finished his rousing rendition of 'Chicken Plucker's Hoedown'. Her smile was grinning from ear to ear with purple berry goo.

"Hey, Roy, I gotcha some pie!" She cackled. "My, this is some fine pie I got here."

The crowd roared with laughter and cheers. Wilda Davis was standing near the front of the stage with her hands held together like she was ready to wish and pray at the same time, jumping up and down. Wilda thought she could recognize the exact berries she had baked into her berry delight pie right on Minnie Pearl's face. Please, please, please, was all she thought. It had to be a vote for her pie – so good, it had to be shared with Roy Clark!

"Does anyone play the banjo? Hey, Roy! Pass over Mr. Magic strings here."

She yelled. A jolly old geezer stepped up and sat on the stool. "Do you know Moonlight in the Woods?" She asked him. He grinned and nodded in the affirmative. "OK then, let's have at it!" With that, Minnie took her index finger and wiped the berry pie off her face just like a windshield wiper on a 55 Chevy. With her finger loaded with purple, she slurped it into her mouth and started belting out her song. The old geezer strummed mightily on the banjo and looked longingly at Minnie Pearl as if she were his true love. She played it up too, massaging his shoulders. Mussing up his curly hair, running her finger under his chin. All the while the old coot giggled enjoying every moment. Roy Clark just stood and ate his pie with a smile on his face.

"Best gig, I ever had!" he told a bystander.

Meanwhile, James and Julia stood in the café looking out at the crowd. Irma had detected a little secret conversation going on between them. "You want to fill me in, or is this something personal?"

"No, hon, nothing personal. You remember that little lady we saw bring in that humongous pie. The four and twenty blackbirds pie?" James whispered.

"Yes, I do." Irma admitted.

"Well, I can't put my finger on it. But I think I know that woman. She seems really strange but there's something. I've never been here before in my life but I know her. Something about her. I can't put my finger on it. Jules, you're clueless on her, right?"

"Righto! Jimmy!" Julia answered. "Oh, reprieve over. There's Minnie on her way back. Let's get back into position, shall we?"

With the four seated at the table, once again, Kathy brought the next lot of pies. "We're starting the savory meat pies now! Once this category is done, you should be able to start the final judging and crunch your data." Everybody groaned.

"Thank you, Kathy," answered Julia and Irma simultaneously. They looked at the five pies placed before them, in a straight line. James started to slice the first one.

"Maybe we should have started with the savory pies and worked to dessert,"

THE PRICKLEBERRY PIE CONTEST

Irma said, holding her stomach. "The entries are getting heavy now."

"Whoop-ti-doo! Steak and Ale, I believe, just like Mother used to make! Mmmm, thrilling!" James announced with a huge smile on his face.

"The steak's very tender…I like the onions." Julia added.

"Beefy, big enough chunks. The sauce is scrumptious." Irma said.

"I wish I could just swill down a pitcher of the ale sauce. That would hold me 'til Tuesday. Pour a little on my steak and I'd be in heaven," James said as he licked his lips.

"Very flaky crust. I do believe this is just like Mama's lardy crust! Man, that lady could cook!" Minnie Pearl reminisced, "I miss her every day!"

Archie Redman would have been pleased. The judges thought highly of his entry. So much so, it was the leading contender in the savory meat category. And nobody questioned the use of the ale, since none of them knew that this was a dry county.

CREAM CHEESE PASTRY

2 cups flour
Pinch of salt
1 stick butter, room temperature
1 8 oz. pkg of cream cheese, softened
4-6 T. ice water

In a medium mixing bowl, cut in butter and cream cheese with a pastry blender until crumbly. Add ice water a tablespoon at a time, stirring with a fork, until mixture starts to form a dough. When ingredients are all moistened, form into a ball and chill. Yields 1 9" double crust pie or 2 9" pie shells.

FLAKY CITRUS PASTRY

3 cups flour
1 T. sugar
1 tsp. salt
1 T. grated lemon zest
1 tsp. grated orange zest
1 stick of sweet butter, diced into small cubes
½ cup shortening, diced into small pieces
6 T. ice water

In a large mixing bowl, combine the flour, sugar and salt. Add the lemon and orange zest and stir to incorporate. Cut in butter and shortening with a pastry blender until mixture resembles coarse curmbs. Add water a tablespoon at a time, mixing with a fork. Mix lightly just until dough holds together. Form into a ball and chill thoroughly before using. Roll out on lightly floured surface. Yields a double crust 9" pie or 2 9" pie shells.

FLAKY PIE CRUST

2 ½ cups sifted flour
1 tsp. salt
6 T. butter
6 T. lard or shortening
4-6 T. ice water

In a medium mixing bowl, stir together flour and salt. With a fork, cut in butter and lard. Add ice water, continuing stirring with a fork until dough forms. Mold into a ball and chill thoroughly. When ready to use, cut dough in half. Roll out one half on a lightly floured surface making a large circle. Repeat with second half. This recipe will prepare a 9" double crust pie or 2 9" pie shells.

GRAHAM CRACKER PIE CRUST

1 1/2 cups graham cracker crumbs
¼ cup sugar
½ stick of butter, melted

In a medium mixing bowl, mix graham cracker crumbs and sugar together. Using a fork, blend in the melted butter until thoroughly incorporated. Pour into a 9" pie tin. Chill about 1 hour before filling or bake in a preheated oven at 350 degrees Fahrenheit for 6-8 minutes, then remove and cool before filling.

Variation:
Sweet spice: Add 1 tsp. each ground cinnamon and ground allspice to graham cracker crumbs.

Substitute same amount of crushed vanilla wafers for the graham crackers.

Substitute same amount of crushed chocolate wafers for the graham crackers.

GRANDMA'S HOME-STYLE PIE CRUST

1 stick butter, room temperature
1 cup flour
Pinch of sugar
Pinch of salt
2 T. cold milk

In a medium mixing bowl, stir together flour, sugar and salt. Add butter an whisk quickly with a fork. When lightly blended, pour in milk and stir just until thoroughly blended. Form into a ball, cover and chill thoroughly. When ready to use, roll out on a lightly floured surface. This recipe prepares a 9" pie shell.

GREEK STYLE SAVORY PIE CRUST

1 ½ tsp. active dry yeast
½ tsp. sugar
¼ cup warm water
2 ¾ cups all purpose flour, plus more for kneading
1 tsp. salt
1 egg
2/3 cup milk
2 T extra virgin olive oil

Dissolve yeast and sugar in ¼ cup warm water. Let stand for about 10 minutes or until foamy. Combine flour and salt in a large mixing bowl. In a separate bowl, beat egg with milk, olive oil and yeast mixture. Add to flour and stir, forming a soft dough. Turn out onto a floured board and knead for about 5 minutes, until the dough is smooth and elastic. Add extra flour, if needed to keep dough from being too sticky. Shape into a ball and place in a lightly oiled bowl, turning to coat. Cover with a cloth and set in a warm place for about 45 minutes or until dough has doubled in size.

When ready to use, punch down and divide into 2 balls, one slightly larger than the other. This will make enough dough for a 10" pie pan or a 9" by 13" baking dish.

ITALIAN STYLE SAVORY PIE CRUST

2 cups flour, plus extra for rolling
¼ tsp. sea salt
1 large egg
¼ cup extra virgin olive oil
¼ cup warm water

Place flour and salt in a large mixing bowl. Stir lightly with a fork to blend the salt in. Add egg, olive oil, and warm water. Mix with a fork, then knead to form a soft smooth dough. Form into a ball and allow to rest in the bowl. Cover with a towel and chill for one hour before using. This will make enough for a bottom and top crust for a 9" pie.

OLD FASHIONED VINEGAR PASTRY CRUST

1 raw egg
1 T. white vinegar
½ cup ice water
4 cups flour
1 T. sugar
2 tsp. salt
1 13/4 cups shortening

In a small bowl, beat egg lightly, then stir in the vinegar and ice water. Set aside. In a large mixing bowl, combine the flour, sugar, and salt. Cut in shortening with a pastry blender until mixture has the consistency of coarse crumbs. Add egg-vinegar mixture, mixing quickly with a fork to form a dough. Mold into a ball and chill thoroughly. When ready to prepare pie, roll out dough on lightly floured surface. This recipe will yield 2 9-10" pie shells or a double crust pie. The vinegar keeps the pastry tender. This is an old heirloom recipe.

PATE BRISEE

2 sticks cold sweet butter, diced into ½" cubes
1/3 cup + 1 T. ice water
2 ½ cups flour
1 ½ tsp. salt
1 tsp. sugar

In a medium mixing bowl, stir together flour, salt and sugar. Cut in butter until mixture forms coarse crumbs. Add ice water while stirring to form dough. Work quickly. Form into 2 balls, flatten slightly, cover and chill thoroughly. When ready to use, roll out on a lightly floured surface. This recipe will make a 9" double crust pie or 2 9" pie shells.

SCOTTISH OAT PASTRY

1 cup flour
1/3 cup regular or quick-cooking oats
¼ tsp. salt
7 T. butter
2-3 T. ice water

In a medium mixing bowl, stir together flour, oats and salt. Cut in butter until course crumbs form, similar to peas. With a fork, blend in ice water. Form dough into a ball. Roll out on a floured surface. This will fit into a 9" pie pan.

STANDARD PIE PASTRY

2 cups sifted flour
½ tsp. salt
2/3 cup shortening
4-6 T. cold water

In medium mixing bowl, blend flour and salt using a fork. Using 2 knives held together or a pastry blender, cut in the shortening as quickly as possible. As the shortening blends into the flour, it will begin to hold together. When mix blends, it will resemble peas. Start adding water, one tablespoon at a time, continue to blend. When the mixture becomes moist enough to hold together, Form into a large ball, then cut in half/ Form each into a ball and roll out to 1/8 inch thick, into a circle, on a lightly floured surface. Repeat with second ball. Place in pastry pans and bake as directly. This recipe will make 2 9" shells, or enough to make a 2 crust pie.

MARVELLE'S HOT WATER PASTRY

2 cups sifted water
½ tsp. baking powder
½ tsp. salt
1/3 cup boiling water
2/3 cup shortening or lard

Stir together flour, baking powder, and salt in a medium mixing bowl. In a separate bowl, pour boiling water over the shortening or lard and stir with a fork until shortening melts and mixture is creamy. Add to flour mixture and blend into a dough. Form into a ball, cover and chill thoroughly before using. Proceed as for Standard Pastry. This recipe will make 2 single 9" pastry shells or 1 9" double crust pie.

MAMA'S SOUTHERN PASTRY CRUST

2 cups sifted flour
½ tsp. salt
1 cup shortening or lard
6 T. ice water

Blend flour and salt with a fork. Cut shortening or lard into the flour. Add water, one tablespoon at a time, working quickly, to form a dough. Roll out on a lightly floured surface. Handle deftly as this is a rich dough. You may want to chill this dough thoroughly before rolling out to handle easier. This will make enough to make 1 9" double crust pie or 2 9" pie shells.

SWEET RICH PASTRY CRUST

1 cup flour
Pinch of salt
4 T. butter
½ cup powdered sugar
1 egg yolk
2 tsp. water

Combine flour, salt, and sugar. Cut in butter until mixture resembles course bread crumbs. Add egg yolk and water, blending until a firm dough forms.
Form into a ball and cover. Chill for 30 minutes before rolling out.

[16]

THE CLOUDS HAD BUILT UP all afternoon increasing the heat and humidity. Finally, at about 3:20 p.m., it started to rain. The clouds had passed over the square. It was only raining on the opposite side of the highway. Everyone in the square remained dry. It was quite an odd sight.

As the clouds moved east and took with it the rain that could have created a disaster for the festivities, the air freshened and cooled. The late afternoon reduced to the mid-seventies and the breeze seemed to caress everyone in the square. Roy Clark called out a fifteen minute break and declared he needed to get some lunch. His voice now a little croaky as he entered the Chuckwagon Café, asking Kathy to seat him at the table behind the judges.

"Ah'm needing a lunch break. Anyways, I'll be the peanut gallery." He told the judges with a big grin.

"Roy, honey, you do what you need to do. You've had it easier than the rest of us here. Ah'm 'bout ready to explode, myself!" Minnie Pearl assured him. Irma just shook her head in agreement, her mouth filled with pie. Her face looked glazed over.

Kathy removed another group of tastings from the table and brought back the huge three foot diameter pie they had seen earlier that morning. "Last one!

Entry 482!"

The four of them sat staring at the pie. It looked perfect.

"Hoo-wee! That is one big pie!" Minnie Pearl commented. "I don't rightly think I've ever seen a pie so huge."

"Now, Jim," Julia said, "the trick for baking a pie of this magnitude would hinge on whether the center was completely done. If the center is done, the edges could be over-baked. To be fair, I think we'll need to test the center AND the edge. We need consistency here."

James nodded his head in agreement. "I concur 100%. This was really chancey by the competitor. Yet, it looks perfect."

"But does it taste good?" Irma asked. "To me, that is the biggest key right now. I'm not into whether the maker followed explicit instructions from the Culinary Arts Institute or whether it warrants its' own Michelin star due to its' humongous size."

James laughed heartily, "Oh, that's rich! The pie was so big it earned its' own star. Hah-hah!" Suddenly, James' face had that strange look again. He glanced over to the waitress station. He saw Kathy talking on the phone. "Oh, Kathy? When you have a moment, can you tell me who entry 482 is?" She nodded back.

Kathy had called me to report that the judges were now on their last pie sample. As soon as they were finished with it, they would take one last break, then start compiling their grades. I would help them with that task, the least I could do. "Pamela, Kathy just called. They are on their last pie. Let's shut down and lock up."

"That's OK, dear. Go on ahead. I'll clean up and then come over."

"Come on Pamela! We've waited all day for this! Let's help them count the tallies."

"Go on ahead. I'll be along shortly. It's all right, Francine, just go."

"Come on, join in the fun. You need to spend some time with the judges. I think James took a liking to you."

"Like I said, just go on. I'll be there shortly. It wouldn't be fair."

"What wouldn't be fair? Oh…oh Pamela. Did you? I asked you before but you didn't answer me, did you enter the pie contest?" I asked with a smile. "With what? What category?"

Pamela nodded her head and her twinkling blue eyes showed her excitement. "Yes, I did. Now just go. I won't tell you what it is. I don't know if it was good enough. I'm sure they are waiting on you. Go on, now!" She shooed me off with a wave of a dish towel.

"Anything you make is a winner in my book." I said sincerely. I turned the "Closed" sign on the door, then opened it and stepped out locking the door behind me.

The crowd had swelled again in the square. It was easier walking completely around the square than through it to get to the cafe. Once inside, I heard James arguing with Julia over a chicken pot pie. Julia denied it should be classified as a pot pie. It had a French twist. It was "Poulet, James." It had a wine based sauce. Minnie Pearl sided with Julia.

"Chicken pot pie has peas and carrots in it, all in a yella' gravy. Ever'body knows that."

"This chicken pot pie is really a chicken stew. Deep, rich, in a wine sauce laced with mushrooms and lemon thyme. It should be served in a deep dish with a puff pastry on top." Irma fought back.

"Now, now, everyone! Let's stop fighting and start the tallying. Are you all going to spend the night at my place? Because the way it's going, you won't be able to make a decision until tomorrow!" I tried to umpire. I took a clean spoon off the table and dipped into the huge chicken pie. "Wow! That's good. That's better'n good. James, the ladies win the argument. Judges, tally the votes!"

[17]

IT WAS 5:05 P.M. AS Lou Evans stepped onto the stage in the town square. His busboy, Jimmy Boyd, pushed a restaurant cart onto a ramp at the back of the stage leaving it beside Lou as he stood behind the microphone. The cart, itself, held an impressive array of awards from shining golden trophies to white, gold and blue ribbons. The television news teams and press corps took their places in front of the stage to get the best photographs of the judges and the winners as the announcements would be made. The crowd buzzed with excitement.

Kathy and I escorted the judges through the crowd to the stage area. Lou commenced with the official notice that the pies have all been tasted and votes have been tallied. He indicated that the judges are making their way onto the stage. Once he provided the rules of the pie contest, he would again introduce the judges and the winners will be announced.

James instructed the ladies to get on stage first and he would follow them. As Lou spoke, I stepped onto the stage and was followed by Irma and Minnie Pearl. Julia followed them and then stood near the lowest edge of the steps as James ascended them.

"James, you go first, ahead of me. You'll need to give me your hand and help pull me up. I'm so stuffed!"

Suddenly, the stage groaned. A sickening creaking sound emitted from underneath and then an immediate deafening crack. The crowd yelled. I saw Julia slipping off the stairs bashing her knee into one of them. Minnie Pearl and Irma hugged each other as it seemed the stage shuddered and staggered momentarily. When I looked down near the band box, I saw James' head peering from the floor of the stage. He had fallen through. He was actually standing on the ground underneath the stage/band box looking out toward the back of the stage.

"Whoa, Nelly! Help me up!" the big bald head said as it rotated toward the crowd.

"Somebody get me some ice!" Roy Clark yelled as he headed towards the stairs. "Julia Child busted open her knee."

Several men tried pulling James Beard up onto the stage but it was no use. He was far too heavy without the use of an engine winch. Steve Kyper pulled a hammer out of his utility belt and a crowbar magically appeared. Within minutes, Steve had removed the siding of the band box where James could duck slightly and walk out.

"Let me try this again," James said as he walked up the stairs for the second time.

Lou had shifted several people to the opposite side of the stage. It seems there had been too much weight on the one end. "We need to spread out and apportion the weight. It seems like we had quite a load of pie here today."

"Well, folks, it seems I did get my fill of pie today." James Beard announced as he patted his stomach. "I'm sorry for creating a big hole in your band box, but I'll donate enough funds to make it right. Julia, are you alright? My, that girl can sure shovel it in. We all need to thank Minnie Pearl here today. She did an admirable job of testing and voting on the best pies in America and for bringing in her good friend, Roy Clark. Hope you all enjoyed him. Last but not least, please give Irma Bombeck a hand for a valiant job today. Most of you don't know this, but we picked up Irma in Hot Springs early this morning and she had been stung by a honey bee. She sure is sweet and we've enjoyed her being with us today.

"As most of you know, the whole shebang thrown today was due to a very great man. We miss him terribly, Charley Simson. I've known Charley for over twenty-five years and we had good times when we were in New York together. He was a great chef, great restauranteur, overall great guy. When he and his lovely wife, Francine, arrived here in Silent Springs, it was our loss, your gain. I'll let the emcee continue, but I just wanted to let you know how much I love this place, the people have been wonderful to us and to let you all know how much we've appreciated your hospitality. Before we move on, I just want to let you know, I never tasted the finest pies until today. You are all wonderful bakers! Thanks for the opportunity of tasting them all. Roy Clark, thank you again for your music today, always a great showman, and I admit, you win your argument this morning. The South has risen again today with all your wonderful pies!" As James spoke, his eyes glanced across the crowd, then fixed on one woman, Lucky.

Well, now we had reached the time I had been dreading the most. Everyone talking about Charley. True, it was kind of sappy, kind of wonderful. My heart bursting with love and pride but aching to be with Charley. How I wish he could be here today. How I miss him.

"Francine?" Lou asked.

"What, huh?" I said off-handedly. Clearly I was in my own little world, not paying attention. Lou's monologue was just droning somewhere in the background of my mind.

"Francine, I had asked you why Charley always greeted his customers with "Welcome Home". Do you know why?"

"Uh…I don't really. It was just his way of welcoming everybody. He wanted people to feel at home, comfortable, I guess. He said that line from the minute we pulled into town."

"Well, it was always so wonderful to hear him say that. The town board put a petition into the U.S Postal Service. Plus, the petition was approved. I want to let everyone know that as of next Monday morning, the name of our town will be changed from Silent Springs to Welcome Home, Arkansas, in his honor. What do you think of that, Francine?"

I was kind of blown away. Speechless. Then suddenly, the crowd cheered and whistled. They began to chant "Welcome Home, Welcome Home!" Without warning, that same mysterious young man that always showed up in our shop jumped on stage.

"Hold that thought!" he shouted. "Please let me speak!" He said as he grabbed the microphone out of Lou's hand. "A couple months ago, a grave miscarriage of justice took place here. A big mistake happened and I need to let everyone know about this!"

THE PRICKLEBERRY PIE CONTEST

"Son," Lou Evans said "maybe another time. Please give me the microphone."

"No, everyone must hear this!" He said. His voice sounded urgent. My name is Neal. I worked for the County. I was here on the day that the man collapsed and died on the sidewalk over there." He pointed to the spot where Charley had been.

"On the same day, another man collapsed and died too. They were both taken to the same hospital and later moved to Little Rock. Fortunately, I discovered a bit of hope and I'd like to share it with you. The man that collapsed here was Charley Simson. The man that collapsed and died was Charlie Simpson. I think it is appropriate for everyone here to say Welcome Home to this man."

He turned and placed two fingers in his mouth and whistled loudly. Behind the stage, parked alongside the square sat an ambulance. Suddenly the doors opened and the attendants pulled a wheelchair out of the back end.

"There was mistaken identity due to spelling of their names. Because Mr. Simson could not speak for many weeks, we didn't know his name for sure. I'd like to welcome home, Charley Simson!"

The attendants pushed the wheelchair up towards the back of the stage and up the ramp. When the crowd saw the wheelchair, a deafening cheer went up.

"Oh my God, Charley!" I cried. I dropped to my knees on stage. It was him, though he was not physically or mentally too with it. "Charley, my love!"

"Welcome Home, Charley!" the crowd roared.

Shortly thereafter, the ambulance took Charley and me home. We left the festivities to the judges. I really can't remember what happened. All of it some weird bizarre dreamscape. The most important thing was that Charley was alive after all.

[18]

AS YOU CAN IMAGINE, THE rest of the day, for me, was a blur. I had my husband back. In body and spirit, broken, but repairable. We will spend months and maybe years of recuperation but at least we are still together. Thank you, Neal, you wonderful kid, for figuring out there was a problem. Now, I guess, I'll have to call the mortuary on Monday and ask them to pick up Charlie Simpson, whoever he is, from my coffee table in the living room.

I don't even know who won the pie contest or any of the categories. Ruta Mae will be dropping by the list of winners for me. She called to tell me that we sold over twenty-five hundred copies of our cookbook and another fifteen hundred are being printed. She took orders at the little booth she had set up when the cookbooks ran out.

The judges and Roy Clark will all stay with us for a couple of days after the pie contest. Although Charley knows what's happening, his speech therapy will need to continue for a while. He does want to spend some time with them.

What a day! The best day of my life.

[19]

THE CREW TRUDGED IN JUST after nine P.M. in a sunset glow. A happy lot but worn out.

"Oh Francine!" James bellowed out. "We're home! Ladies, have a seat, Roy, you better unnotch your belt buckle and give yourself some room there." He said as they all entered the living room. Each person seemed to repose to a piece of furniture of their choice.

Everyone seemed to have melted.

"Would any of you care for a nice glass of wine? Jim, a scotch on the rocks for you? I'd ask if you want anything to eat but I'm not sure it's wise right now. Four hundred and eighty-two pies! How do you have any room? If you do want something, now or later, please help yourself. I don't want to overstuff you. Take your shoes off and make yourself at home. By the way, Charley's asleep. We've had such an emotional afternoon, I'm sure he'll be out until morning."

I took the orders and moved to the kitchen. I could hear banter and laughter. All I wanted to do was to go to bed and snuggle. I wasn't feeling particularly festive. I am ecstatic that Charley is alive and home but I know that we have a long road to recovery. It's quite overwhelming to say the least.

When I entered the living room with the tray of drinks and passed them out, each one gave me a hug. I started to break down. I was trying hard to be a good hostess.

Julia spoke first. "We know this has been a remarkable day, for you, for us. I think the best thing to do is to just go to bed. All of us just want to veg out and talk a little before we do the same thing. I think we're all a little miserable. Too stuffed to be comfortable right now. I think I'll call Paul even though it's nearly midnight, his time. I miss him."

"That's right, honey. You go on and leave us be. We can keep company tomorrow morning. Julia has promised to make us omelets for breakfast." Minnie Pearl winked.

"We plan on doing a lot of talking in the morning and spending time with Charley. We're going to help you assess his needs and work on getting the treatment he needs. Plus support you. You might be worried about him and his condition, but you are the one that needs the most help right now." Irma said.

"We will be here for you."

"The ladies are right, Francine. We can talk about all that in the morning. Plus, I'll give you the blow by blow on the contest happenings, what you wanted to know and probably some you didn't." Roy chimed in. "I was there in the thick of things. Some of it wasn't pretty."

"If you or Charley needs anything overnight, wake me up for help." Irma said.

"Me too,!" Minnie Pearl added.

"Go on, darling, and get some shut-eye." James piped in.

I extended my nighty-nites and excused myself. I heard James ask Roy if he still could play something tonight.

"Are your fingers sore?" Roy responded that he still had it in him to play acoustic guitar. "Great," James said, "Something soft. Some serenade, for the kids…"

The last thing I recalled while laying there in bed with Charley was the breeze blowing in from the windows, caressing our faces, and the soft strain of "Some Enchanted Evening".

[20]

DAWN ARRIVED SOONER THAN I expected. Actually, I was completely unaware that it was morning, until the phone rang. I woke up and looked at the clock, 8:30 AM, it said. I reached for the phone and found Pamela on the line. Oh heavens, I've overslept!

"Good morning dear!" She said cheerfully. "I took the liberty of opening up for you this morning, a lot of work ahead of us today. I brought my granddaughter, Shelby, in to help. I figured you would be indisposed. I assumed that you will be spending time with your husband today and getting him situated. We can get everything baked and in order. I'll touch base with you later."

"Oh Pamela, that would be great. I'm so sorry that I'm not there this morning. I actually overslept!" I turned over with the phone in my hand and saw Charley looking at me. Oh my gosh, my husband is actually here. "I'll come in later. Pamela? Thank you again. You've been so good to me! I really appreciate it."

How I could have overslept and also forgot that my husband was home in bed with me was just amazing. "Oh, Charley, honey…" I leaned closer and kissed him.

The house was quiet and we laid in bed, basking in the joy of being together. Charley's mobility was limited. It took some time for me to maneuver him into the wheelchair next to the bed. Exhausting. We rolled into the kitchen and found Irma, Minnie Pearl and Julia sitting at the table having coffee. Breakfast was long gone, although the omelet pan was still sitting on the stove waiting for the next order.

"Oh, I thought everyone was still sleeping. I'd still be sleeping if Pamela hadn't called me." I apologized to the group. "Is James up?"

"Oh, yes, honey, he's long gone." Irma responded. "Said he had something to do and would be back later this morning. Can Julia make you an omelet for breakfast?"

"That would be wonderful. Not many people can say they've eaten omelets made personally by Julia Child. What a treat, huh, Charley?"

Charley smiled and grunted. Speech therapy was definitely going to be a priority along with physical therapy. Julia placed the hot plate in front of us on the table. Charley and I shared the wonderfully fluffy omelet. I gave him a forkful, then took one myself. Before we knew it, the omelet was gone. As we ate, I told Charley about everything that had happened while he was in the hospital. I explained to him that I had to delegate the cookbook to Ruta Mae. I brought out the copy that I had left on my nightstand.

"Look at this, Charley…" I said as I turned the pages slowly.

HISTORICAL

Velma Smackover's clean white sheets waved in the breeze on her clothes line. "I'm blinded by the bright, Mrs. Smackover!"

"Honey, that's because of the bluing." She answered. "My mama always used bluing on her whites. It makes them bright white. Also, I love drying clothes on the line. The sun and fresh air does wonders for your laundry. They are stiff though. Sometimes my husband's shirts are taken off the line like boards. Many women take pleasure in ironing as well. There is a lot of pride and used to be a lot of competition in doing laundry. Could you imagine hanging your laundry on a line, let's say in New York City, where everyone could see your laundry? As a woman, you wanted to make sure that you did a good job in cleaning clothes or your reputation could be tarnished. You don't have to worry about it so much here in the country. Every woman tended to do laundry on the same day. Monday was wash day. Surely, you did not go visiting on wash day. A proper lady did not want to see someone's laundry, nor would you want someone to look at yours."

"Wow, Mrs. Smackover. I never gave it much thought before. I guess I never had to worry about doing laundry. Actually, my mom still does mine." Ruta Mae admitted, her face blushing pink.

"Lordy, my mind a-wanders sometimes. Once a teacher, always a teacher. As you know, I'm retired now. I miss it now and again. I surely didn't mean on giving you a whole dissertation on laundry."

"Mrs. Smackover, I think if I had had a teacher like you, I would have liked school more. I'm sorry you were gone before I reached high school. I would have enjoyed your class."

"I would have loved to have you, honey. Let's go on in and I'll get you my pie entries."

BEAN PIE

1 cup small dry white beans
¾ cup melted butter
¾ cup granulated or brown sugar
2 eggs
½ tsp. salt
½ tsp. cinnamon
½ tsp. nutmeg
1 tsp. vanilla
5 drops yellow food color
1 unbaked 9 inch pie shell

Rinse beans and pick out any small stones or other debris. Place beans in a large mixing bowl and cover with four cups of water. Soak beans overnight. Drain beans and rinse again. Place in a large pot and cover with 1 quart of water. Bring to boil, then lower heat and cook until beans are tender. Drain and press beans through a sieve or puree in a blender. Place mashed beans in a mixing bowl and add the melted butter and sugar. Stir until blended. Beat in eggs, one at a time. Add salt, cinnamon, nutmeg, vanilla and food color. Beat until smooth, then pour into prepared pie shell.

Bake in a preheated 350 degree Fahrenheit oven for 45 minutes or until knife stuck in center comes out clean.

AMISH BOTZELBAUM PIE – SOMERSAULT PIE

The dough and the filling will flip-flop during baking.
1 unbaked 9" pie shell
For dough –
1 cup sugar
¼ cup lard
1 egg
½ cup sour milk
1 ¼ cups flour
½ tsp. baking soda
For Filling –
½ cup sugar
1 tsp. ground cloves
1 tsp. cinnamon
1 T. flour
1 egg, beaten
½ cup molasses
1 cup water

Set aside the 9" pie shell. Preheat oven to 350 degrees Fahrenheit. Take two separate mixing bowls. In the first bowl, mix the dough ingredients in the order given. In the second bowl, mix the filling ingredients in the order given. Put the dough ingredient mixture into the prepared pie shell. Then carefully, pour the filling mixture over the dough mixture. Bake for 35-40 minutes until top is golden brown.

BROWN SUGAR PIE

A 1 pound box of light brown sugar
4 large eggs
¼ cup milk
2 tsp. vanilla
Pinch of salt
1 stick of butter, melted
1 prepared pie shell

Preheat oven to 325 degrees Fahrenheit. In a large mixing bowl, beat eggs slightly, then add the whole box of brown sugar. Mix in the milk, vanilla and salt. Stir until smooth, then add the melted butter. Pour into the pie shell. Bake pie for 1 hour.

BUTTERMILK PIE

1 ½ cup sugar
3 T. flour
6 T. melted butter
3 large eggs, beaten
1 ½ cups buttermilk
1 tsp. vanilla
¼ tsp. nutmeg
1 prepared pie shell

Preheat oven to 325 degrees Fahrenheit. In a large mixing bowl, stir together the sugar and flour. With a fork, blend in the melted butter, then add the beaten eggs. Stir in the buttermilk, vanilla and nutmeg. Pour into the prepared pie shell. Bake for 1 hour, 15 minutes.

CHESS PIE #1

¼ cup butter
½ cup sugar
1 cup firmly packed brown sugar
Pinch of salt
3 eggs
1 tsp. vanilla
2 T. flour
½ cup cream
1 cup chopped pecans
1 T. apricot jam
1 unbaked 9" pie shell

Preheat oven to 375 degrees Fahrenheit. Cream butter, add the sugars and salt, blending well. Add eggs, one at a time, beating well after each addition. Stir in vanilla, flour, and cream. Make sure mixture is smooth, then add pecans. Brush bottom of pastry shell with apricot jam. Pour filling into pie crust. Bake pie for 45-50 minutes or until a knife inserted in center comes out lean. Do not overbake.

CHESS PIE #2

6 T. butter
2/3 cup granulated sugar
2/3 cup packed light brown sugar
Pinch of salt
2/3 cup buttermilk
½ tsp. grated nutmeg
1 egg at room temperature
4 egg yolks
1 prepared 9" pie shell

Heat oven to 325 degrees Fahrenheit. In top of a double boiler over medium heat, whisk the sugars, salt, buttermilk, nutmeg, egg yolks and egg. Add the butter, stirring frequently. Continue to cook, about 5 minutes. Mixture should be smooth and warm. Remove from heat and allow to cool for 5 minutes. Pour into pie shell. Bake for 45-50 minutes or until center is set. Cool before serving.

GREEN TOMATO PIE

6-8 medium smooth-skinned tomatoes, cored and sliced
1 T. lemon juice
½ cup each firmly packed light brown sugar, granulated sugar, unsifted flour
½ tsp. each salt, ground cinnamon, grated nutmeg
4 T. butter
Cream
Pastry for a 2 crust 9" pie

Preheat oven to 425 degrees Fahrenheit. Prepare pastry for bottom of pie pan. Prepare lattice top.

In a large bowl, place sliced tomatoes and sprinkle with the lemon juice. Stir so that the lemon juice is mixed in. In a separate bowl, combine the sugars, flour, salt, spices and butter. Blend together, forming a crumbly mixture.

Starting with crumb mixture on bottom of pie pan, layer the crumbs and tomatoes. End with tomatoes on top. You should have about 4 layers total.

Form lattice top over the tomatoes. Brush lattice with cream.

Bake for 20 minutes, then reduce temperature to 375 degrees and continue baking for about 45 minutes.

Variation:
Rather than slicing tomatoes, cut into dices. Combine with the lemon juice. After blending the crumbs together, add the tomatoes, stir together and pour into the prepared pie shell. Bake as directed.

GWETCHA PIE — AMISH PRUNE CUSTARD

1 unbaked pie shell
5 T. granulated sugar
1 heaping tablespoon flour
2 eggs, beaten
½ cup cream
½ cup prune juice
2 ½ cups cooked prunes, chopped
Cinnamon

Preheat oven to 350 degrees Fahrenheit. In a small bowl, combine the sugar and flour. Sprinkle half of the mixture into the prepared pie shell. In a separate bowl, combine the beaten eggs, cream, prune juice and the remaining sugar-flour mixture. Blend well. Add the chopped prune and pour the custard into the prepared pie shell. Sprinkle cinnamon on top. Bake for about 40-45 minutes until the custard is set.

MAGIC LEMON CUSTARD PIE

1 ½ cup sugar
2 T. butter, melted
1/3 cup flour
Pinch of salt
Zest from 1 lemon
5 T. lemon juice
3 large eggs, separated
1¼ cups milk
I unbaked 9" pie shell

Preheat oven to 375 degrees Fahrenheit. In a large bowl, stir together the sugar and butter, blend in the flour, salt, lemon zest and lemon juice. In a small bowl, beat the egg yolks and blend in the milk. Stir into lemon mixture.

In a medium bowl, beat egg whites with an electric mixer on high speed until stiff. Gently fold in the egg whites into lemon mixture. Carefully pour filling into pie shell. Bake on lowest rack for 50-55 minutes or until top is richly browned. Center should feel set when lightly pressed. Let cook on a rack. Serve at room temperature.

MAPLE SYRUP PIE #1

5 T. cornstarch
Pinch of salt
1 cup milk
2 cups maple syrup

2 eggs, separated
4 T. sugar
1 9" baked pie shell

Preheat oven to 350 degrees Fahrenheit. In a small bowl, blend cornstarch and salt with a small amount of milk to make a slurry. In a medium saucepan, heat remaining milk and maple syrup to boiling. Add cornstarch slurry. Cook mixture for 5 minutes over low heat, stirring constantly. In another small bowl containing the egg yolks, beat until smooth. Pour a small amount of the maple syrup mixture into the egg yolks, beating constantly, then pour into the saucepan with the maple syrup mixture. Stir thoroughly, remove from heat. Allow mixture to cool for 5 minutes. Pour mixture into prepared pie shell. Beat egg whites until stiff but not dry. Gradually add the sugar and beat until very stiff. Top pie with meringue. Bake pie for 15 minutes or until meringue is golden brown.

MAPLE SYRUP PIE #2

1 ¼ cups light brown sugar
½ cup whipping cream
1/3 cup maple syrup
1 extra large egg
2 tsp. butter, soft
1 partially baked 9" pie shell

Preheat oven to 350 degrees Fahrenheit. Blind bake pie shell for 15 minutes, then remove from oven and set aside to cool.

Using an electric mixer, in a large bowl, beat sugar, whipping cream, maple syrup, egg, and butter, until smooth. Pour into pie shell. Bake until crust is golden brown and filling is set, about 45 minutes.

MAPLE SYRUP PIE #3

Pastry for single crust pie
4 eggs
1 ½ cups maple syrup
¾ cup packed brown sugar
½ cup light cream
½ tsp. vanilla
½ tsp. ground allspice
Pinch of salt

Preheat oven to 50 degrees Fahrenheit. Blind bake pie shell for 5 minutes, then remove from oven and allow to cool.

In a large bowl, beat eggs with mixer, blend in remaining ingredients, just until smooth. Pour into partially baked pie shell. Place pie in oven and immediately turn down temperature to 350 degrees. Bake for 30 minutes or until a knife inserted in center comes out clean.

OATMEAL PIE

4 eggs
2/3 cup granulated sugar
1 cup packed brown sugar
2 T. butter, softened
1 tsp. vanilla
½ cup each of rolled oats, shredded coconut and chopped pecans
1 unbaked 8" pie shell

Preheat oven to 375 degrees Fahrenheit. In a large mixing bowl, beat eggs, the gradually add the sugars, blending well. Beat in the butter and vanilla. Stir in the oats, coconut and pecans. Pour into prepared pie shell. Bake for 35 minutes.

THE PRICKLEBERRY PIE CONTEST

OSGOOD PIE

½ cup butter
1 cup sugar
3 eggs, separated
1 cup chopped pecans
1 cup chopped pitted dates
½ cup golden raisins
Pinch of salt
1 unbaked 9" pie shell

Preheat oven to 325 degrees Fahrenheit. Cream butter and sugar together. Beat in the egg yolks, blending well. Fold in the pecans, dates, raisins and salt. In a separate bowl, beat egg whites until stiff. Fold into the fruit and nut mixture. Turn out into the prepared pie shell. Bake for 45 minutes.

SHOOFLY PIE

¾ cup water
¾ cup dark molasses
1 small egg, beaten
1/3 tsp. baking soda
1½ cups flour
½ cup packed light brown sugar
½ tsp. baking powder
Pinch of salt
1 T. + 1 tsp. shortening
1 unbaked 9" pie shell

Preheat oven to 375 degrees Fahrenheit. In a small saucepan, heat water until just warm. Add molasses, stir until blended. Remove from heat, cool slightly, then vigorously whisk in egg and baking soda. Set aside.

In a large bowl, mix together flour, brown sugar, baking powder and salt. Blend in the shortening. Mixture should resemble course meal. Set aside.

Pour molasses mixture into pie shell, then top with crumbly mixture. With a butter knife, swirl through without touching bottom pie crust to lightly blend.

Bake for about 45 minutes or until top is a lightly colored and crust is golden.

SHAKER LEMON PIE

3 whole lemons, sliced paper thin and seeded
2 ½ cups sugar
6 eggs, beaten
Pastry for a 9" double crust pie

Mix the sliced lemons with the sugar, cover, refrigerate and let macerate for at least 12 hours.

When ready to prepare pie, preheat oven to 450 degrees Fahrenheit. Lay pastry crust on bottom of pie pan and prepare lattice for top.

Remove lemon slices from refrigerator and mix in beaten eggs. Pour into pie shell. Cover with lattice top.

Bake at 450 degrees for 10 minutes, then reduce heat to 350 degrees and continue baking for another 30 minutes.

SORGHUM PIE

1/3 cup sugar
3 T. flour
1 tsp. ground nutmeg
Pinch of salt
3 large eggs

¾ cup sorghum or molasses
½ cup milk
2 T. butter, melted
1 ½ tsp. vanilla
1 prepared pie shell

Preheat oven to 325 degrees Fahrenheit. In a small bowl, blend the sugar, flour, nutmeg and salt together. Set aside. In a medium mixing bowl, beat the 3 eggs, then add the sorghum and milk. Blend until smooth. Add the dry mixture and stir well. Add the melted butter and vanilla. Pour into the prepared pie shell. Bake for 1 hour.

JEFF DAVIS PIE #1

3 T. flour
1 cup sugar
1 tsp. cinnamon
1 tsp. cloves
1 cup milk

3 eggs
1 cup cream
2 T. butter
1 tsp. vanilla
1 9" baked pie shell

Combine flour, sugar, cinnamon and cloves. Stir in milk slowly to keep the mixture smooth. Separate 2 eggs and set aside the whites for meringue. Combine 2 egg yolks with the whole egg and blend with a fork until smooth. Add cream and mix well. Stir into flour and sugar mixture and cook over hot water until thickened, stirring constantly. Remove from heat and add the vanilla. Cool slightly, then pour into the baked pie shell.

Make meringue of reserved egg whites and ¼ cup sugar. Spread over pie and bake in a preheated 350 degree oven until the meringue is delicately browned.

JEFF DAVIS PIE #2

1 ¾ cups sugar, divided
1 T. flour
1 /2 cup butter
1 cup heavy cream
2 large eggs

4 large eggs, separated
¼ tsp. nutmeg
Pinch of salt
1 prepared pie shell

Preheat oven to 325 degrees Fahrenheit. In a double boiler over medium heat, combine 1 ¼ cups of the sugar, flour, butter, heavy cream, 2 eggs and 4 egg yolks, nutmeg and salt. Constantly whisk, cooking mixture for approximately 10 minutes. Mixture should be thick and smooth. Remove from heat and allow to cool for 5 minutes.

In separate mixing bowl, beat 4 egg whites until stiff. Add the remaining ½ cup sugar and beat until very stiff.

Pour filling to pie shell. Top with meringue. Bake for 35-40 minutes or until knife inserted comes out clean.

VINEGAR PIE #1

1 cup apple cider vinegar
2 cups water
1 cup packed brown sugar
2 T. butter
½ cup flour

Prepare pastry crust for 9" pie, bottom and lattice crust

Line a pie pan with the pastry shell. Prepare lattice and set aside. Place pie shell in the refrigerator to chill while you prepare the filling. Preheat oven to 450 degrees Fahrenheit.

Combine vinegar, water and brown sugar in a saucepan. Bring mixture to a boil and cook for 3 minutes. Add butter and stir until it has melted. In a small bowl, mix flour with enough water to make a smooth paste. Stir slowly into the butter syrup and cook, while stirring constantly, until filling is thick and smooth. Pour into chilled pie shell. Place lattice crust on top. Place in hot 450 degree oven and bake for 10 minutes, then reduce heat to 350 degrees and continue baking for 25 minutes.

VINEGAR PIE #2

1 ½ cup granulated sugar
½ cup butter, melted
3 large eggs, slightly beaten
Scant ¼ cup apple cider vinegar
1 tsp. vanilla
1 prepared pie shell

Preheat oven to 325 degrees Fahrenheit. In medium mixing bowl, blend sugar and melted butter together. While stirring constantly, add one-third of the eggs until blended well, then add another third and the remainder. Mixture should be smooth. Add the apple cider vinegar and the vanilla, blending well. Pour into prepared pie shell and bake for 1 hour.

NUTS

Ollie and Marvelle Farmer live in a comfortable small two-toned clapboard house. The top half is colored a weathering white, the bottom has been painted leaf green. The roof has been replaced, over the years, by sheets of galvanized metal that sings when it rains into a soothing melody. The dwelling is surrounded by tall green pecan and walnut trees, the umbrella shade from the trees keep the home reasonably cool in the summer heat. It looks idyllic.

"Hey, ya'll! Come on in." Marvelle yells from her rocker on the covered front porch. Ollie stands ramrod straight then bends over to help Marvelle get up out of her seat. "Ah'm a little stiff this morning." She explained.

We enter the house through the front door into a quaint living room. The walls are covered with family photographs, framed crewelled bible verses and prints of wild and domesticated animals. The furniture is covered in crocheted afghans and colorful cotton quilts, some worn and well used. All confirming a comfortable existence from a previous hardscrabble lifetime.

"Ollie, please take the pies to the gal's car. And, be careful with 'em." Marvelle instructed. "Do you have a few minutes? Ah'll pour us some nice iced tea. Have a seat, will ya?" Marvelle turned and opened the small refrigerator and removed a pitcher of cold tea which she placed on the kitchen counter. Her arm reached into a cabinet and took out three jelly jars. Ollie returned to the kitchen with a small bucket of ice, turning it so that ice cubes rolled out into each of the glass jars. The tea was poured and we clinked our jelly jars together.

"Cheers! Good luck to you, Miz Farmer!" I took a sip. The tea was pure tasting, cold, sweet and satisfying. "I hope you don't mind me asking, but why did you want to enter the Prickleberry Pie Contest?"

"Not a'tall! Well, ah haveta say that them folks at the grocery have done a lot for our town, fixed it up and all. That said, ah've always had the same, what you call philosophy, about makin' things better. Ah thinks it's important that we all support people in positive ventures. Sad that the fella, Charley, passed on, though. We should all lend the poor lady some support. She has to carry on his plans. That must be really tough. Like Ollie and me in the early days. Right after we married, we bought this place with my dowry. Soon after, the Great Depression hit and we had some tough days. Many times ah thought we'd lose our farm. Then one day, ah sold some of my wedding presents for pennies on the dollar and invested them in chickens. Some people thought ah had lost my mind. Ah raised them chickens and sold the eggs. While many folks around here thought it was only pocket change, it kept my apron full. Ollie and ah were pretty lucky. We got through the hard times ok, ain't that right?"

"Yes, mam!" Ollie shook his head in agreement.

"Anyways, baby girl, I put Marvelle's pies on the floorboards of your car. Drive safely, ya hear? They need to arrive in prime condition. Every nut in those pies comes from those big trees you see out in the yard."

"Really? Mr. Farmer, what kind of nuts do you grow here?"

"Why, well we have snap pecans, hickories, walnuts and the legendary black walnuts out there."

"Oh. Is there a difference? I mean, do they taste different?"

Ollie guffawed and bent over. He rose choking and laughing, slapping his left thigh. Marvelle grinned changing the format of her roadmap face. " Honey, let me get you a taste of all four. You can make up your own mind." She got up from the kitchen chair and pulled canning jars out of her freezer. She plucked a nut from each one. "They'll thaw out in just a minute with the warmth of your hand. Ah keep them in the freezer this way so they don't get wormy." Her flat thin palm offered the samples.

"Wow…Wow…ooooh wow! My gosh, they're all different, that's for sure! Oh, wow, the time! I gotta go. Thank you so much, Miz and Mister Farmer, for your hospitality."

"Well, thank you, honey, for stoppin' by and picking up the pies. Drive safely now, they're prize winnin' pies in there." Ollie said as he pointed to the car. "Make sure you ask the judges for a taste test. You'll see how good Marvelle's are."

FRENCH STYLE ALMOND PIE

Prepared puff pastry to cover a double crust 8" pie
1 cup granulated sugar
1 cup almond meal flour (finely ground almonds)
Zest of 1 large orange
Zest of 1 lemon
1 tsp. orange extract
1 tsp. orange flavored liqueur, such as Triple Sec or Cointreau
1 egg yolk
1 T. water
Powdered sugar from sprinkling

Preheat oven to 400 degrees Fahrenheit. Take puff pastry, enough for just pie shell, onto a lightly floured board and roll out to 1/8 inch thick. Place in pie pan, trim edges and chill in refrigerator.

In a medium mixing bowl, combine the sugar and almond flour meal until blended. Add the orange and lemon zests, the orange extract and the orange flavored liqueur. Stir to blend thoroughly. Pour mixture into prepared pie shell.

Take second puff pastry and roll out as before. When 1/8" thick, take rolling pin and drape pastry over it. Moisten prepared pie shell, then drape the second pastry over. Trim and crimp edges with a fork, sealing the filling in. Take a sharp knife and lightly score top being careful not to cut completely through the pastry. Score intersecting lines forming a grid pattern on the pastry top. Chill pie for 30 minutes.

Remove pie from refrigerator. Make an egg wash with the egg yolk and water. Brush across the top of the pastry crust. Immediately, place in hot oven and bake for approximately 40 minutes. Top should be puffy and brown. Remove from the oven. Sprinkle about 2 T. of powdered sugar over the top. Using kitchen torch or a hot broiler, heat top until the sugar has melted and formed a glaze.

TRADE WINDS MACADAMIA NUT PIE

1 9" unbaked pie shell
1 bag of macadamia nut pieces
1 2 oz. bottle of crystallized ginger
4 eggs
1 cup brown sugar
1 cup dark corn syrup
¼ cup dark rum
¼ cup melted butter

Preheat oven to 450 degrees Fahrenheit. In a small bowl, mix the macadamias and ginger together, then pour into the prepared pie shell.

In separate mixing bowl, beat eggs and brown sugar together. Add dark corn syrup and dark rum, beating well. Add melted butter, then pour into pie shell over the nuts.

Bake for 10 minutes, then reduce temperature to 325 degrees and continue to bake for 30 minutes or until center of pie is set.

MACADAMIA PIE

1 9" unbaked pie shell
½ cup sweet butter, softened
¾ cup firmly packed light brown sugar
¾ cup light corn syrup
¼ cup honey
4 eggs, beaten
1 tsp. vanilla
1 6 oz. bag chopped macadamia bits

Preheat oven to 425 degrees Fahrenheit. In a large mixing bowl, beat butter and brown sugar until light and creamy. Beat in the light corn syrup and honey, then blend in the eggs and vanilla. When thoroughly blended, stir in the macadamias. Pour into prepared pie shell.

Bake in hot oven for 10 minutes, then reduce heat to 325 degrees and continue baking for another 30 minutes or until top is golden brown.

PEANUT BUTTER PIE

2 8" unbaked pie crusts
3 eggs, beaten
½ cup sugar
1 cup white corn syrup
3 T. butter, melted
½ cup peanut butter, smooth or crunchy

Preheat oven to 350 degrees Fahrenheit. In a large mixing bowl, place beaten eggs, then beat in sugar, corn syrup, melted butter and peanut butter. When thoroughly blended, pour into the prepared pie shells. Bake for 30 minutes.

MARVELLE'S BEST PECAN PIE

1 9" unbaked pie crust
3 eggs, slightly beaten
¾ cup light corn syrup
¼ cup unsulphered molasses
1 cup sugar
1 tsp. vanilla
2 T. butter, melted
2 cups pecan halves

Preheat oven to 350 degrees Fahrenheit. Pour pecan halves into pie shell and smooth to evenly distribute. Set Aside.

In a mixing bowl, place slightly beaten eggs, then add remaining ingredients, mixing thoroughly. Pour over pecans. Place in oven and bake for 50-55 minutes or until center is set.

CHOCOLATE NUT PIE

1 9" prepared pie shell
1 cup semi-sweet chocolate chips
3 eggs, slightly beaten
½ cup firmly packed light brown sugar
½ cup light corn syrup
2 T. melted butter
1 tsp. vanilla
2 cups unsalted nuts, any variety or combination

Preheat oven to 375 degrees Fahrenheit. Sprinkle chocolate chips in bottom of pie shell. Then sprinkle nuts on top of the chocolate chips and set aside. In a mixing bowl, beat together the eggs, brown sugar, and corn syrup. When blended, stir in melted butter and vanilla. Pour over the chocolate chips and nuts. Bake for 45-50 minutes or until golden. Cool before serving.

OH-SO-GOOD PIE

1 9" unbaked pie shell
¼ cup butter, softened
1 cup sugar
3 eggs, slightly beaten
¼ cup light corn syrup
1 tsp. vanilla
½ cup milk chocolate chips
½ cup chopped pecans
2 T. bourbon

Preheat oven to 375 degrees Fahrenheit. Cream butter and sugar together. Add eggs, corn syrup and vanilla. When well blended, add milk chocolate chips, pecans and bourbon. Pour into prepared pie shell. Bake for 45 minutes.

SOUTHERN SAWDUST PIE

1 cup sugar
1 cup flaked coconut
1 cup chopped pecans
1 cup graham cracker crumbs
5 egg whites from extra large eggs, unbeaten
1 8" unbaked pie shell
Whipped cream
1 can mandarin oranges, drained or 1 banana, sliced

Preheat oven to 350 degrees Fahrenheit. In a large mixing bowl, combine the sugar, coconut, pecans, graham cracker crumbs and egg whites. Mix well by hand, do not beat. Turn into prepared pie shell. Bake for 35 minutes or until filling is just set. Do not overbake. May be served warm or at room temperature. To serve, top each slice with a dollop of whipped cream. Place a few mandarin orange segments or banana slices on top.

BLACK WALNUT PIE

1 8" unbaked pie shell
3 large eggs, slightly beaten
1/3 cup firmly packed light brown sugar
1 cup dark maple syrup
1 tsp. apple cider vinegar
1 tsp. vanilla
Pinch of salt
2 T. sweet butter, melted
1 cup chopped black walnuts

Preheat oven to 375 degrees Fahrenheit. Spread the black walnuts evenly on the bottom of the pie shell and chill.
In a large mixing bowl, place eggs and beat in the brown sugar until smooth. Beat in the maple syrup, apple cider vinegar, vanilla and pinch of salt. When blended well, add the melted butter. Pour mixture into the prepared pie shell. Bake for 35 minutes.

THE PRICKLEBERRY PIE CONTEST

GERMAN CHOCOLATE PIE

1 9" pastry crust, partially blind baked
1 cup firmly packed light brown sugar
½ cup light corn syrup
½ cup dark brown corn syrup
¼ cup butter, melted
3 large eggs
1 ½ tsp. vanilla
Pinch of salt
2 cups pecan halves
¾ cup semisweet chocolate chips
1 ½ sweetened flaked coconut

Prepare pie crust, lay in pan and trim. Blind bake for 10 minutes, then set aside.

Preheat oven to 350 degrees Fahrenheit.

In a large mixing bowl, combine the brown sugars and both corn syrups. Add the eggs, beating well. Then add melted butter, vanilla pinch of salt. Stir in the pecans.

In the lightly cooled pie pan, sprinkle the chocolate chips evenly on the pie shell. Sprinkle the coconut on top of the chocolate chips. Pour and spread the filling on top of the coconut. Bake for 1 hour or until center is set.

HOLIDAY

Every Thanksgiving spurred a heated pumpkin pie baking contest in the Wage household. The competition between Mama and her three daughters was fierce. Yet, the rules and the outcome was always the same. Start with Aunt Grace's recipe, which was really the famous canned pumpkin company's and bake the best-looking and best-tasting pie. Everyone in the family looked, tasted and voted for the winner. The oldest daughter took her freshest extra large Rhode Island Red eggs and changed the sweet spices, doubling the cinnamon and matching it with an equal amount of allspice. She liked it strong spicy-sweet. The ingredients had to be mixed in a certain order and then poured into her prepared Southern Pie shell which baked at a high temperature, then lowered until the custard was set. She always made a second pie in the same fashion but added a small kick of fine sippin' whiskey. The men always appreciated that.

    The middle daughter's inspiration was to win by utilizing natural and organic ingredients. Everything from scratch, the way the Pilgrims must have prepared it. She started by taking a small sugar pie pumpkin, hollowing it out and laying it in a baking pan. The pumpkin was roasted then pureed for use. She used fresh eggs from her Pekin ducks which offered a higher though some of the family found it to be a slightly rubbery custard filling. She finessed the sweet spice by adding freshly ground ginger and nutmeg to her cinnamon and cloves. She often added a small amount of finely ground fresh black pepper and substituted honey for the sugar the recipe called for. She poured it into a prepared whole wheat pie shell and baked it until it was firmly set.

    The youngest daughter followed the instructions on the can of pumpkin to the best of her abilities. After the pie was baked and cooled, a split opened up in the center and the pie began to sweat. She began to cry and in a fit of rage, threw the pie away in the trash and announced she didn't know how to cook. She conceded defeat to her oldest sister whom she adored and whose pies she preferred above all others anyway.

Meanwhile, Mama, who had perpetuated the pie baking competition year after year, was under such stress, always forgot to add the spices to the pumpkin at the right time. Just as she went to pour the custard into the pie shell, she remembered. She stirred the spices in as best she could. She baked the pie and realized, once again, that the spice had separated and floated back to the surface, creating a freckled top. Another defeat on record and now looking forward to next year to try again.

The moral of the story: Despite good intentions, sometimes things go awry. Just accept the flaws and move on rather than dwelling on them. There's nothing worse than a holiday getting ruined by a trivial pursuit.

AUNT GRACE'S PUMPKIN PIE

2 eggs
2 cups canned pumpkin
¾ cup sugar
½ tsp. each of salt, ground ginger and cloves
1 tsp. cinnamon
1 2/3 cups evaporated milk
1 9" prepared pie shell

Preheat oven to 400 degrees Fahrenheit. In a large mixing bowl, beat eggs slightly. Stir in the pumpkin, sugar, salt and spices. Blend well. Add the evaporated milk, blending well. Pour into a 9" pie pan lined with the pie crust. Bake in 400 degree oven for 35-40 minutes until custard is set. Knife inserted in the center should come out clean.

THE BEST STANDARD PUMPKIN PIE

2 large eggs, slightly beaten
1 16 oz. can of pumpkin
¾ cup sugar
A pinch of salt
1 heaping teaspoon each of ground cinnamon, ground allspice and ground cloves
1 12 oz. can evaporated milk
1 prepared 9" pie shell

Preheat oven to 425 degrees Fahrenheit. In a large mixing bowl, slightly beat the eggs. Add pumpkin to the eggs and beat to incorporate. Add sugar, salt and spices. Blend in well. Pour in the can of evaporated milk and stir until blended. Pour into pie shell. Place in preheated 425 degree hot oven and bake for 15 minutes. Reduce heat and continue baking for an additional 45 minutes or until custard is set. Inserted knife should come out clean.

Variation: Southern Spiked – add 2 T. fine sipping whiskey to egg/pumpkin mixture. Proceed as directed above.

ITALIAN STYLE EASTER PIE

For crust –
2 cups flour, plus extra for rolling
2 large eggs
Pinch of salt
¼ cup extra virgin olive oil
½ cup water
1 tsp. baking powder

For Filling –
¾ lb. combination of Italian style cold cuts, chopped, such as capocollo, mortadella, pepperoni, prosciutto, salami, or soppressata

1 lb. fresh ricotta cheese
¾ lb. combination of Italian style cheeses, chopped, such as asiago, fontina, mozzarella, parmesan, or provolone
5 eggs
Fresh ground pepper
A few sprigs of Italian flat leaf parsley, chopped
A few leaves of fresh basil, torn

Preheat oven to 325 degrees Fahrenheit. Prepare pie crust by placing the flour on a floured board. Sprinkle the mound with the baking powder. Mound up and put a well in the center. Add the 2 eggs, pinch of salt, and olive oil. Using a fork, work the wet ingredients into the flour until dough forms. Add extra flour if necessary. Knead dough until smooth and form into a ball. Allow to rest for 30 minutes.

In a large mixing bowl, combine the meats and cheeses, mixing well. Add 4 of the eggs, black pepper, parsley and basil.

Cut dough in half and roll out into circles. Fit one circle into a 8" pie pan. Add filling to pie pan. Top with second circle. Press and seal edges well. Beat remaining egg in a small cup. Brush onto top of pie. Cut a few slits in top to release steam. Bake for 45-50 minutes or until filling is set and crust is browned.

Allow to cool to before serving. This should be served at room temperature.

OLD FASHIONED MINCEMEAT

2 cups finely chopped or grated tart apples
Juice and finely grated zest of 1 lemon
Juice and finely grated zest of 1 orange
1 cup apple cider
1 cup dark brown sugar
½ cup golden raisins
½ cup currants

¼ tsp. each cinnamon, ground cloves, and nutmeg
¼ cup finely chopped candied citron, candied lemon peel, candied orange peel or candied cherries 2 T. brandy
1 T. dark rum
Milk for brushing
Sugar for sprinkling

Prepare mincemeat filling up to 2 weeks before using. Put the apples, juices and cider in a Dutch oven. Mix and over medium heat, bring to a boil. Reduce heat and simmer for 10-15 minutes. Stir in the brown sugar, lemon and orange zest, spices, raisins, currants. Cook for another 10-15 minutes. Remove from heat and add the candied fruit. When completely cool, add the brandy and dark rum. Pack into a large glass jar and refrigerator until needed.

To prepare pie, preheat oven to 450 degrees Fahrenheit. Make sweet pastry crust for top and bottom. Line a 9" pie pan with pastry crust, place filling in and cover with top. Press edge to seal well. Brush top with milk and sprinkle with sugar. Place in preheated oven and bake for 10 minutes. Reduce heat to 350 degrees and continue baking for 45 minutes.

Variation:
Traditional mincemeat – add ¼ cup finely chopped beef suet and ½ cup finely chopped beef from chuck roast to apple mixture and cook as directed above.

CHRISTMAS NESSELRODE PIE

2 cups cooked chestnuts, divided
Syrup from 1 small jar of maraschino cherries
3 cups milk
Pinch of salt
1 ½ cups sugar
5 eggs, divided
2 cups heavy cream, whipped

THE PRICKLEBERRY PIE CONTEST

¼ cup pineapple juice
¼ cup pineapple chunks
¼ cup maraschino cherries, drained
½ chopped candied fruit
1 9" pie pan prepared with graham cracker crust

Take 8 cooked chestnuts, broken into small pieces and soak overnight in the maraschino syrup. First make a custard by scalding milk in top of a double boiler. In a medium size mixing bowl, beat salt, sugar and 5 egg yolks together until light. Add milk gradually, stirring constantly. Move mixture back into the top of the double boiler. Cook over medium heat until mixture has thickened. Strain through a sieve and allow to cool.

Take the remaining cooked chestnuts, and press through a sieve. You will need 1 ½ cups. In medium mixing bowl, whip cream until stiff, set aside. In a separate mixing bowl, take egg whites and whip until stiff.

To cooled custard, carefully fold in the pineapple juice and chestnut puree. Then fold in the whipped cream and whipped egg whites. Fold in the fruits and remaining nuts, drained from syrup. Fill pie shell with mixture and place in freezer. Freeze until firm before serving.

SWEET POTATO PIE

2 ½ cups cooked mashed sweet potatoes
2 T. melted butter
2 eggs, slightly beaten
¾ cup sugar
Pinch of salt
1 tsp. ground cinnamon
½ tsp. ground nutmeg
Grated zest of 1 orange
1 cup milk
½ cup orange juice
1 9" prepared pie shell

Preheat oven to 400 degrees Fahrenheit. In a large mixing bowl, combine mashed sweet potatoes and melted butter. Add beaten eggs and incorporate them well. Add sugar, salt, spices and orange zest.

Stir them in well. Add milk and orange juice. Pour into prepared pie shell. Bake in preheated oven for 15 minutes, then reduce temperature to 350 degrees. Continue baking for 30 minutes or until firm.

Can decorate finished pie by placing toasted pecans halves around edge, sprinkle shredded sweetened coconut around edge or sprinkle top with marshmallows.

Toast marshmallow-topped pie in a hot oven until lightly browned.

Variations:

Coconut – delete orange zest and orange juice. Substitute milk with 1 ½ cups coconut milk.

Rum – Follow recipe as directed. Add ¼ cup dark rum and 1 tsp. vanilla to mixture when the milk is added.

SAVORY

Kayla Sanders was considered the luckiest person in Silent Springs. Although life has thrown her a few bones, she never felt especially privileged. Starting out with modest means, fortune generously shone on her as she grew.

"Hi, Kayla! I'm Ruta Mae. I'm here to pick up your pies for the Prickleberry Pie Contest."

"Oh, great. Thanks so much for picking them up. I couldn't leave the Realty Office. I'm the only one here right now." Kayla said. She stood up and moved towards the kitchenette area of her Realty Office. She is tall and lanky. Her pink three piece suit reminiscent of Chanel styling, seems out of place. She moves gracefully as she carries her pies. "Here you go! This one here," she pointed, "is my Crying Pie."

"Crying Pie? Why do you call it that?"

"Well, you'll probably think I'm crazy. It's an onion and cheese pie. When I used to feel sad and melancholy, I'd make it. I didn't want anybody to know that I felt depressed or anything. If somebody asked me why I was crying or why my eyes were all red and teary, I'd blame it on slicing all the onions." She said with a smile on her fair face. "When they knew I was making this pie, they were so happy since it is so wonderful. Lots of flavor. And then I'd cheer up."

"Kayla, why would you feel so sad? Everybody thinks you're the luckiest person in town."

"Well, you're probably too young to remember, but, I was kind of adopted by the Wardlows. I grew up in a small coal town in Pennsylvania. I'll never know for sure, but I think my Mama was mighty unhappy there. She abandoned me and my Daddy. She just left one day without any notice. We never could find out what happened to her. I was just a little girl then but it left me with some guilt. For years I thought she left because of me. It was all my fault.

My Daddy didn't take it too well. He had a temper and was kind of known as a tough guy. Plus, he nursed his sorrows out with drink. After a while, I think, he was in trouble at work and he probably lost his job, but I didn't know that for sure. Eventually, he got caught by the police for some petty crimes and they took him away. By then, I was fifteen. I got a job as a waitress in the little café down on the corner. I paid the rent and took care of myself. Nobody knew my Daddy was gone. Nobody asked and I didn't offer any information. I was afraid the authorities would take me away too."

"Wow, Kayla, what happened, then?"

"One day, I was working at the café and the Wardlows came in. I served them lunch. Mrs. Wardlow, Muriel, was very nice. She talked to me sweetly and told me that they were on vacation. They were driving to Hershey, Pennsylvania in their new convertible. She told me that on the way home, they'd stop in again and bring me some chocolate.

True to their word, they returned about a week later. Again, I served them lunch. It was very slow at the café and we didn't have any other customers. They asked me about my life and although I didn't want to tell them anything, they offered me a chance to go with them. At the last minute, I agreed. They took me to my little apartment above the café, took my photos of my parents, my little T.V. and some clothes.

So, I came to Silent Springs with them where they raised me like their own daughter. The Wardlows were well to do, you know. They never had any children of their own. Woody owned the only Realty in the County. Soon after we arrived here, Muriel really was in poor health. She had always had a housekeeper and cook to help her. I was her adopted daughter and constant companion. When I graduated high school, the Wardlows suggested that I go to secretarial school. Woody paid my way and when I graduated, I went to work for him in the real estate office. After a couple years, Muriel passed on. Right after that, Woody let Lettie, the housekeeper, go after nearly thirty years of service. Woody was quite a character as you may remember. He had wild white hair, always puffing a cigar and loved his whiskey. He was never a stranger to controversy. A lot of people didn't like him, but if you needed a real estate transaction, there wasn't anyone else.

One day, he recommended that I get my real estate license. He said it was about time I learned the business completely and cover for him. Golf, cardplaying, going to casinos and whatever else became his priority. I did what he asked. You know, Woody was always a gentleman to me. He treated me upright like a father. There was never any impropriety. But people in the town talked. They always thought he brought me in to be his bimbo. It took quite a few years to overcome all that myth and rumor.

In the end, one day, Woody lost his life wrapping that big convertible around a power pole down on Highway 59. In his will, he left everything to me, the money, the house, the business, everything. Most people think I'm lucky because I inherited all this, but in the end, there was one thing that I never was able to acquire, at least not yet, and that's love. So, when I feel a little down, I make myself the Crying Pie that Lettie taught me how to bake."

"Wow, Kayla, I feel kinda sad after hearing all that. I hope you find yourself a boyfriend. You're really pretty and really smart. Anyway, your pies smell great and I hope you win in your categories. If you ever want to do something, call me, OK?"

"That'd be very nice. Don't worry about me, Ruta Mae. I feel blessed."

THE CRYING PIE

4 strips of bacon, diced
5 cups thinly sliced onions
1 cup grated swiss cheese
2 tsp. sugar
1 T. flour
½ tsp. salt
Dash of cayenne pepper
¼ tsp. each coarsely ground black pepper and ground nutmeg
3 eggs
1 cup milk
1 9" unbaked pie shell

Preheat oven to 425 degrees Fahrenheit. In a large frying pan, fry diced bacon until crisp, then remove from pan and set aside. To same frying pan, sauté the onions in the bacon fat until soft and light golden. Turn heat off. Sprinkle swiss cheese over the onions and stir around.

In a small bowl, combine sugar, flour, salt, cayenne, black pepper and nutmeg. In a separate bowl, beat the eggs lightly. Add the seasoning mix, then stir in the milk. Place sautéed onions in pie shell. Sprinkle with bacon. Pour egg and milk mixture over the onions. Bake in preheated oven for about 35-40 minutes or until custard is set and golden brown.

Variation:
Substitute swiss cheese with a sharp cheddar cheese.
Substitute the bacon with ½ cup diced cooked ham.
Substitute nutmeg with same amount of dried thyme.

HORTOPITTA – GREEK STYLE ASSORTED GREENS PIE

For shell, prepare Greek style dough for a 2 crust pie
1 lb. of assorted mixed greens – use combination of swiss chard, spinach, escarole, endive, dandelions, all washed well
1 T. extra virgin olive oil
3-4 large green onions, finely chopped
1 T. finely chopped fennel fronds
1 T. finely chopped fresh dill weed
1 T. finely chopped fresh parsley leaves
1 cup feta cheese, finely crumbled
¼ cup milk
¼ tsp. each of salt and finely ground black pepper
2 large eggs, beaten
2 T. uncooked long grain rice

Bring a large pot of water to a boil. Add the greens, return to a boil and cook only for 2 minutes. Drain greens and plunge into a bowl of ice water. Drain again, squeezing out any moisture. Place on cutting board and finely chop greens. Place in a large bowl and set aside.

In a large frying pan, heat olive oil over medium heat and fry the green onions, fennel, dill weed and parsley for about 2 minutes or until softened. Turn into the bowl of chopped greens. Add the feta cheese, milk, salt and pepper. Mix well. Blend in the beaten eggs and uncooked rice.

Preheat oven to 350 degrees Fahrenheit. Roll out pie crust into 2 circles. Take a 9 or 10" pie pan and lightly oil. Place bottom crust in. Add pie filling and smooth for an even pie. Top with crust, pinching edges to form a tight seal.

Bake in a preheated oven for 45-50 minutes or until crust are crisp and golden.

Variation:
Replace the feta cheese with an equal amount of parmesan.
For a milder cheese flavor, replace feta with an equal amount of cottage cheese or ricotta.

Substitute greens with 8-10 fresh leeks, cleaned, trimmed, and split lengthwise. Slice. Delete green onions, fennel fronds, feta cheese, milk. Increase olive oil to 2 T., parsley to 1 cup and fresh dill to 1/3 cup. Add 1 T. finely chopped fresh mint, 1 T. lemon juice, ½ tsp. grated lemon zest. Begin by sautéing leeks in olive oil about 10-12 minutes or until tender. Remove from heat and place in a large mixing bowl. Add remaining ingredients, stirring well to incorporate. Pour into pie shell and follow further instructions.

ITALIAN STYLE SPINACH OR SWISS CHARD PIE

Prepare Italian Style Pie Dough for 2 crusts
2 lbs. fresh spinach leaves or swiss chard, washed well
3 large eggs
½ cup freshly grated parmesan cheese
½ tsp. each salt and black pepper
¼ tsp. ground mace
Healthy pinch of red pepper flakes
Olive oil for brushing

Preheat oven to 350 degrees Fahrenheit. Bring a large pot of water to a boil. Cut stems from spinach or any very large stem ends from the swiss chard and discard them. Rinse leaves once again and place into the boiling water. Allow to cook for 2 minutes, then drain and plunge into ice water. Drain again, squeeze moisture from leaves, then place on cutting board and chop. Set aside.

In a large mixing bowl, blend eggs, parmesan, salt, pepper, mace and red pepper flakes. Add spinach or swiss chard, stir well to incorporate.

Pour into prepared pie shell. Cover with top crust, pressing edges in well and crimping to seal well.

Prick top with a few decorative holes to vent steam. Brush crust with olive oil. Bake in preheated oven for about 45 minutes, or until golden brown.

Variation:
Place 8 T. good quality olive oil into a large frying pan, and heat. Add 2 garlic cloves, sliced thinly and cook until garlic is lightly browned. Be careful not to burn. Remove garlic from pan. Add the spinach or swiss chard and cook for about 1 minute, until the leaves wilt. Remove from frying pan and place in a colander to drain and cool. Proceed with recipe as directed above.

YE OLDE ENGLISH BEEF AND STOUT PIE

1 standard pastry crust with the addition of ½ cup shredded sharp cheddar cheese
3 slices bacon, diced
1 lb. small brown mushrooms, cleaned
1 box pearl onions, peeled and trimmed
Salt and pepper to taste
1 medium size beef chuck or round roast, trimmed and cut into 1" chunks
1 cup flour
¼ cup salad oil
2 large garlic cloves, minced
2 T. tomato paste
1 16 oz. bottle of stout
1 ½ cups full flavored beef broth
2 T. steak sauce
1 lb. each carrots and small red potatoes, peeled and cut into chunks
1 tsp. dried thyme
1 bay leave

THE PRICKLEBERRY PIE CONTEST

In a Dutch oven, fry diced bacon until crisp and remove from pot. Set aside.
Add the mushrooms, onions, and salt to the pot and cook until onions are tender, about 10 minutes. Sprinkle with black pepper to taste. Remove to a bowl and set aside.

Season flour with salt and pepper and dredge beef chunks in flour. Turn heat to medium. Add half the oil to the Dutch oven and add one half of the beef, searing until golden brown. Cook for 5-7 minutes, then remove and add to bowl with the mushrooms and onions. Add small amount of water to the pot, scraping browned bits up, pour mixture into the beef bowl. Add the remaining half of salad oil and cook remaining beef as directed above. Remove from pot. Add small amount of water and again, scrape up bits and pour into beef bowl. Turn heat down slightly. Add tomato paste and garlic, stirring constantly for half a minute, then add stout, beef broth and steak sauce. Stir until blended. Add bacon, beef and mushroom mixture with all the juices. Add carrots, potatoes, thyme and bay leave. Cover pot and allow to simmer for 2 ½ hours, stirring occasionally. Beef should be tender.

Preheat oven to 400 degrees Fahrenheit. Remove bay leave from pot. Roll out pastry dough into large circle, enough to cover Dutch oven and slightly drape over the edge. Using rolling pin, roll up dough and place over pot. Push dough down onto filling. Trim draped edge to 1" and crimp to seal. Cut decorative slits on top. Bake for 35-40 minutes or until crust is golden brown.

Variations:
Substitute 1 bottle of stout with 2 cups of dry red wine.

Add 1 cup frozen peas to beef mixture and stir in, just before putting on top crust.

Add 2 cups peeled parsnips, turnips or rutabagas, cut into chunks. Add with the carrots and potatoes.

Add 2 stalks of celery, cleaned and sliced, when adding the carrots and potatoes. Add 1 cup fresh green beans, cut into 1 ½" lengths to mushrooms and pearl onions. Saute in the bacon fat as directed.

Add 1 cup frozen corn to beef mixture and stir in, just before putting on top crust.

To make potpies, use miniature pie pans or ramekins. Spoon filling into pie pans or ramekins, top with crusts, seal and crimp. Place pie pans on baking sheets. Bake for 30 minutes or until crust is golden brown.

For pasties, make extra pie dough, cut into 6" diameter circles. Spoon filling into center and fold one edge over. Seal and crimp well. Place on baking sheets lined with parchment paper. Bake in preheated oven for 30 minutes or until pasties are golden brown. Cool slightly before removing from sheet.

PORK POTPIES

3 ½ lbs. boneless pork roast
Salt and pepper to taste
2 T. salad oil
1 garlic clove, minced
2 large carrots, peeled & diced, divided
4 stalks celery, diced, divided
1 medium onion, chopped
1 medium sized rutabaga, peeled and diced
1 large russet potato, peeled and diced
2 cups dry white wine
½ tsp. caraway seeds
2 T. grainy mustard
6 T. flour
4 cups full flavored chicken stock
1 tsp. dried thyme
Chopped fresh parsley

Prepared pie dough for 2 covered pies or 2 package of frozen puff pastry Prepare filling by trimming off fat and cutting pork roast into ½" cubes. Sear meat with salt and pepper. In a Dutch oven, heat salad oil over medium high heat. Working in batches, brown meat on all sides. This should take about 5 minutes per batch. Remove meat and place in a large bowl. Add small amount of water to pot and scrape up browned bits, pour into meat bowl. Repeat until all meat has been cooked. On last batch, add garlic, 1 cup each of the carrots and celery, the onion and ¼ cup of the wine. Stir while cooking until wine evaporates. Continue to cook vegetables for a few more minutes until they are soft. Add the remaining wine and continue to cook, stirring occasionally. Allow wine to reduce by half. In the meantime, in a small bowl, combine the caraway seeds, mustard, flour and ½ cup of broth, then whisk it into the pot. Bring to a boil, stirring constantly. Add the remaining broth, pork and juice, thyme, bay leaf. Reduce heat to a simmer and continue to cook, covered about 1 ½ hours, or until pork is tender.

While pork is cooking, if planning on using pie crust, prepare dough and cut into a dozen circles to cover the miniature pie pans. If using puff pastry, preheat oven to 325 degrees Fahrenheit. On a lightly floured surface, work with 1 sheet of puff pastry at a time, roll out to 1/8" thick. Using a 3 ½ " fluted round cutter (for ramekins) or size to accommodate your miniature pie pans. Bake pastry rounds on parchment lined baking sheets for 15 minutes, or until golden brown. Allow to cool.

When pork is tender, add remaining vegetables. Allow mixture to return to a boil, then reduce heat and simmer for another 20 minutes. Vegetables should now be tender. Remove bay leaf, season with salt and pepper, stir in chopped parsley. Divide into 12 ramekin or miniature pie pans. Place on a rimmed baking sheet.

Place 1 puff pastry round on each ramekin or cover pie pans with pie crust. Press to edges and crimp to seal. Bake until pastry is golden brown and juices are bubbling, about 20-25 minutes. Miniature pie crusts should take longer, about 30-35 minutes.

Variations:
When pork is tender, add 1 cup of finely shredded green cabbage with the remaining vegetables. Add 1 tsp. paprika. Follow instructions

as directed. When pork is tender, add 1 cup of finely shredded brussel sprouts with the remaining vegetables. Follow instructions as directed. Substitute the dry white wine with equal amount of beer. Place filling in 10" pie pan or a 9" by 13" baking pan, cover with pie crust or puff pastry (baked). Bake for 45 minutes or until crust is golden brown and filling is bubbly.

TOURTIERES – CANADIAN STYLE MEAT PIES

Enough flaky pie dough for 2 full size pies
1 lb. ground beef
1 lb. ground pork
1 cup fresh breadcrumbs
1 cup finely chopped onion
½ cup water
1 tsp. salt
½ tsp. ground cinnamon
¼ tsp. ground black pepper
¼ tsp. ground nutmeg
Pinch each of ground cloves and ground allspice
1 large egg, lightly beaten

Prepare pie crust. Preheat oven to 350 degrees Fahrenheit. To make meat filling, in a large mixing bowl, combine ground beef, ground pork, breadcrumbs, onion, water and seasonings. Mix well.
On a lightly floured board, roll out pastry dough into 8 circles. Line 4 4" tart pans or miniature pie pans with 4 of the circles. Mound meat filling into each of the pans, mounding up the filling in the center. Moisten rims with water and press remaining pastry crusts on top of each pie. Press firmly around the edges into a smooth rim to seal. Cut slashes on top of each to vent steam. Remaining dough can be cut into decorative shapes and placed on top. Brush tops with beaten egg.
Place tourtieres on rimmed baking sheet and bake in preheated oven for 50-60 minutes or until pies are golden and meat juices run clear.

COUNTRY STYLE TAMALE PIE

1 lb. lean ground beef
1 large onion, chopped
2 garlic cloves, minced
1 11 oz. can corn with mixed red and green bell peppers
1 15 oz. can creamed corn, divided
2 T. masa harina
1 15 oz. can diced tomatoes with puree
4 green onions, sliced
2 tsp. salt, divided
2 T. chili powder
1 tsp. ground cumin
1 small can sliced black olives
1 cup yellow corn meal
4 cups water
1 ½ cups shredded cheddar or Monterey jack cheese

Preheat oven to 350 degrees Fahrenheit. In a large frying pan, brown ground beef. Break up meat as it cooks until crumbly. When lightly browned, add chopped onion and garlic and continue cooking until onions are soft. To pan, add corn with peppers, half of the creamed corn, masa harina, tomatoes, half of the salt, chili powder and the cumin. Stir and allow to cook over low heat. While the meat is cooking, prepare the topping. In a large saucepan, bring 3 cups of water and the remaining salt to a boil. Combine the remaining cup of water with the cornmeal. Pour this mixture into the boiling water, stirring constantly. As mixture begins to thicken, add the remaining creamed corn. Continue to cook over low heat for 3 minutes, then remove from heat. Stir in half of the grated cheese.

Immediately add the green onions, sliced black olives and remaining half of the grated cheese to the meat mixture. Pour meat mixture into a 9" by 13" baking pan. Smooth so that surface is even. Top meat mixture with the cornmeal mixture and again. Spread evenly to form a smooth top. Bake in a preheated oven for 30 minutes.

Variation: Add ¼ cup diced pickled jalapenos to the cornmeal mixture before baking.

SAVORY TOMATO "PIE" A LA JULIA

1 package puff pastry
1/3 cup Dijon mustard
2 garlic cloves, minced
2 cups chopped tomatoes, drain to reduce juice
1 medium sweet onion, chopped
1 cup chopped fresh parsley
1 ½ cups swiss cheese, cut into ½" cubes
Sea salt and freshly cracked black pepper

Preheat oven to 425 degrees Fahrenheit. On a lightly floured surface, roll out 2 sheets of puff pastry to a thickness of ¼". Place on a greased baking sheet. Try to "mesh" the two sheets together. Bake for 15 minutes until lightly golden. Remove from oven and allow to cool for a few minutes.

Combine garlic, tomatoes, chopped onion and parsley in a medium size bowl. Smear Dijon mustard on the puff pastry evenly. Sprinkle tomato mixture over the Dijon mustard, then sprinkle cheese cubes on top. Return to the oven and immediately reduce temperature to 375 degrees. Continue to bake for 20-25 minutes until cheese has melted and begins to lightly brown.

FAMILY CHICKEN PIE

1 stewing chicken
1 tsp. poultry seasoning
½ tsp. garlic powder
½ tsp. salt
½ tsp. black pepper
2 top stalks of celery containing the leaves
4 large carrots, peeled and diced
4 stalks celery, diced
1 onion, chopped
2 large potatoes, peeled and diced
2 T. butter
2 T. flour
2 cups chicken broth
2 T. sherry
1/2 tsp. thyme
2 T. chopped parsley
½ cup frozen peas

THE PRICKLEBERRY PIE CONTEST

Prepared pie crust, prepared biscuit dough, sweet potato crust, country white bread, or buttered breadcrumbs

In large pot, place stewing chicken and cover with water. Season with poultry seasoning, salt, pepper, garlic powder, and 2 top stalks of celery. Bring water to a boil, reduce heat to continue at a simmer. Cover pot and allow to cook for one hour. Chicken meat should be tender. Pull chicken from pot and allow to cool.

Pour chicken broth from pot and measure out 2 cups. Discard celery tops. In same pot, over medium heat, melt butter and add vegetables. Stir. Vegetables should sweat slightly. Sprinkle flour over the cooking vegetables and stir to avoid causing any lumps. Cook for a minute or so, then add chicken broth, sherry and time. Allow mixture to cook, liquid will reduce.

In the meantime, remove skin from chicken and pull meat from the bones. Cut meat into bite-size pieces. Add chicken to vegetables, stir to blend. Add parsley and frozen peas. Check for seasoning. Place mixture into a baking pan. Top. If using pie crust, cover pie with pastry dough, cut a few slits in the top and brush with beaten egg. If topping with baking powder biscuits, place biscuit dough on top, brush with melted butter. If topping with bread, use country white bread (1" thick for Texas Toast), trim crusts off, brush with melted butter. If topping with sweet potato crust, bake 1 sweet potato (enough to have 1 cup) until soft, scrape from shells, add 1/3 cup melted butter, ½ tsp. salt, 1 cup flour and 1 tsp. baking powder and 1 egg. Blend with a fork to form a dough. On a floured board, roll out ¼" thick and cover the chicken pie. If using buttered breadcrumbs, top pie with about 1 cup. Spread over top to evenly distribute. Bake in a preheated 425 degree Fahrenheit oven for 15-20 minutes until topping is golden brown.

NORTHERN WATERS FISH PIE

4 cups cold cooked white fish, such as halibut, cod, sole, flounder, tilapia, smoked finnan haddie, smoked whitefish or your choice
4 slices bacon, diced
1 large onion, chopped
½ tsp. curry powder
½ tsp. ground black pepper
1 bay leaf
2 T. butter
¼ cup flour
1 cup milk
½ cup reserved fish broth
¼ tsp. paprika
2 large potatoes, peeled, quartered lengthwise, then sliced thin
½ cup frozen peas
1 tsp. minced pimento
1 T. finely chopped parsley
Pie pastry to cover 8-9" casserole dish

In large saucepan, place boned, skinned fish of your choice. Cover with water. Season with salt. Water should taste a little salty. Simmer on low heat until fish is cooked through. Remove fish from broth. Place on plate and allow to cool. When cool, flake fish into bite-size chunks. Reserve a half cup of fish broth.

In stew pot, place diced bacon. Over medium heat, fry bacon until just crisp. Remove from pot and reserve. To pot, add onions and allow to cook until golden. Onions should be soft and tender. Add curry powder, black pepper and bay leaf. Stir to coat the onions with the seasonings. Add butter and allow it to melt. To flour, add paprika and stir through to mix. Sprinkle flour into onion mixture and stir well. Cook for 1 minute. Add milk and fish broth, then stir in potatoes and reserved bacon. Continue cooking, stirring occasionally. Allow sauce to thicken. When sauce has reached the consistency of gravy, add frozen peas and pimento. Remove bay leaf. Heat through. Preheat oven to 375 degrees Fahrenheit.

Add reserved fish and fresh chopped parsley to potato mixture. Stir to incorporate. Turn into greased casserole dish. Lay pie pastry over casserole dish allowing it to drape over edge. Trim dough allowing an inch to drape over edge. Press down over top and seal to edge of casserole. Cut a few slits in top to release steam. Place in preheated oven and bake for 35 minutes or until pastry crust is golden brown.

Variations:

Hot Curry–Delete bacon. Saute chopped onions in 2 T. salad oil. Increase curry powder to 1 tablespoon, add ¼ tsp. cayenne pepper, ½ tsp. mustard seed. Delete paprika, pimento and parsley. Add 2 large carrots, peeled and diced, and 1 cup halved small cauliflower florets to the sliced potatoes. Add ½ cup coconut milk to the regular milk and fish broth. Proceed with directions.

Scandinavian Style – replace curry powder with ¼ tsp. ground mace. Substitute pimento with ½ tsp. chopped dill weed. Add 1 cup small peeled, deveined pink shrimp to the fish chunks when adding to the stew.

South of the Border–Substitute bacon with 1 cup chorizo sausage, diced into ¼" cubes. Add ½ cup diced bell pepper and 2 minced garlic cloves to the onions. Substitute curry powder with same amount of ground cumin. Add ½ tsp. chili powder and ½ tsp. garlic powder. Delete bay leaf. Replace butter with olive oil. Replace flour with same amount of masa harina. Substitute potatoes with 2 cups chopped tomatoes. Add 1 cup charred, skinned and sliced mild green chilies, ½ cup sliced green onions. Substitute parsley with fresh chopped cilantro.

[21]

THE GLOW ON CHARLEY'S FACE said it all. He clutched the cookbook against his chest. The phone rang and it was Lou. He was on his way over. Charley's eyes lit up. Obviously, he was happy that he'd be seeing his good friend again. Irma put on a fresh pot of coffee in preparation. We all sat around the kitchen table talking about trivialities until Lou showed up.

Suddenly, the kitchen door popped open and the large figure blocked the sunlight coming in. "Hey, y'all!" James said, laughing. "I'm talkin' southern!

Pretty good for a New Yorker, huh?"

"Oh, Jim, you're such a character!" Julia responded. "Perhaps, you've found a new calling. Beard on Southern Cooking, how about that? Think about it. There's plenty of fodder here to work with."

"Good!" Charley managed to say. "Help."

James patted Charley on the shoulder. "That's right, buddy. We could team up and work on it together. What a project that would be. I'd probably put on another hundred pounds. Yesterday, I ate enough pie to last a year. Whew! I honestly thought I'd explode last night. All thanks to you."

"You're not the only one." Minnie Pearl offered. "Ah hate to admit it, but my stomach was mighty swelled up when we got home. Ah thought my nightgown would burst open." She said as she patted her midriff. "I'd die a thousand deaths in embarrassment, Francine, if you had to clean that up. Lace danglin' from the light fixture, lil patches of flannel hangin' off the bedstead and drapery rods. What a mess!"

"Oh, Lord! I couldn't fathom seeing you without a stitch of clothing, Sarah. I think I'd go blind." James laughed.

"You'd go blind, all right, when I'd poke your eyes out. She said. "Nobody sees me naked and lives to talk about it."

"I hate to admit it," Irma added. "I was afraid I would get sick in the night and keep everyone up. My brain kept thrumming 'cher-ries…cher-ries…cher-ries' all night long. My stomach was spinning around and around. I can't remember when I actually fell asleep.

Charley seemed to enjoy the conversation. He watched intently. We've had a few good laughs this morning. "Does everyone feel OK, today? Just want to make sure." I asked the group. They all agreed simultaneously. "By the way, James, what were you up to this morning? When you left the house, where did you go?"

James Beard explained that he had solved the mystery of Lucky. When her name was called, he suddenly realized who she was. She is actually Carmela Borazine-Crowder, the most well-known culinary historian. She was living here en obscuro due to a famous European scandal that was publicized in the New York Times. She had been accused of being involved with a collaborator working on a large work which plagiarized a sourcebook. While she was eventually cleared of any wrong-doing, she felt her reputation had been tarnished. She fled Europe and decided that she would need to live in anonymity until the dust settled. Silent Springs, Arkansas would be her home until she felt comfortable getting out again. A distant relative offered her living quarters, a modest run-down clapboard house on the edge of town. It was the humongous pie that gave James the clue in the end. He recalled reading the article about the recipe. Maybe he has a new career – James Beard, food detective.

James had run out at the crack of dawn to seek her out and meet with her. I was shocked to discover who she really was. Even Charley shook his head up and down. He knew who she was. Obviously, we had never seen a picture of her but we had read about her for years. Boy, will Pamela be surprised.

"Hey, y'all! We're comin' in." We heard Roy Clark's voice as the front door opened. Roy and Lou stepped into the house.

"We're here in the kitchen. Come join us. Charley's with us." I yelled.

"I'm glad you all are here together. I wanted to thank everybody for their participation yesterday. It went pretty smooth except for that stage collapse." Lou said.

Charley looked at him with a quizzical look.

"Julia? How is your knee this morning?" Lou asked as he looked down at it. It had scabbed over. The edge of Julia's skirt fell just above the abrasion.

"It's fine, Lou. I'll live." She laughed. "When I slipped, I was more worried for Jimmy than myself. All I could see was his head. I guess to the crowd it looked like we were serving Jimmy's head on a platter." Everyone got a good laugh out of that.

"That happened so quickly, it was like I slipped down a rabbit hole. I was standing there thinking for once I had eaten too much and the next thing I know, my feet are on the ground. It took a second to realize that I had gone down. I was looking at your feet. That's when I turned around and faced the crowd. What a gas!" He chuckled.

"Well, Mister Beard, we're relieved that the both of you are all right. I was so concerned all night long. Did everybody survive the portions? You sure ate a whole lot of pie yesterday." Lou expressed sincerely.

Minnie Pearl piped up. "You got that right, mister! Ah never ate so much pie in my life. We were jes' talkin' before you got here that it was a pretty painful night. Roy, how're yer throat and fingertips? Are they raw or blistered?"

"No, I'm good. Irma here, lent me her throat spray and massaged my fingertips last night with some mighty-fine lotion she has. Gotta say, though, I'm glad I'm here and not at home. I'd get an awful razzin' from the boys if they smelled that flowery potion. Thanks again, Irma. It really helped me."

"I'm glad I could help. Charley, Francine, Lou…" Irma started. "Speaking for myself and I'm sure for Minnie Pearl, Julia, James, and Roy, I'd like to thank you for inviting us here. This was quite a challenge on several counts. Charley, you don't know this, but it started out bad. It was hard for us to come, I'll have to admit. We were still grieving for you. We thought you had passed away. To honor you, of course, was important for all of us. Plus, we needed to give Francine our support. Then, in Hot Springs, I was stung by a bee yesterday and had an allergic reaction. We taste-tested 482 pies. That was painful. Luckily, none of us got sick. Lou, no offense, but us Yankees have an inane distrust. I have to admit, and I think I can express this for all of us, that we have been overwhelmed. Overwhelmed with hospitality, overwhelmed by the enthusiasm, overwhelmed with the turnout, overwhelmed that we have Charley again. I'm just plain overwhelmed. Thank you, every one. I think I'm fork tender now. As much as I'd like to stay and help out, I need to go home to Ohio. I have a television appearance to prepare for. Also, being here, I've been impressed on a number of levels. I've decided this morning to write a book. I just thought of the title, 'Life is just a bowl of cherries'. I think I've just been inspired."

"Well, good for you, Irma." Julia said. "I have to admit that I was pretty excited to go on a road trip with Jimmy and come here. Jimmy, you've been the perfect gentlemen. We've had a lot of fun. Irma, I know how you feel. I miss Paul. I've never been away from him this long before. Charley, you know I'd do anything for you, but your lovely wife, Francine, can do all of it and more. My next season starts and I, too, have the need to prepare a new book. Simca has written me and she may come to visit.

"You all go on home. I plan on stayin' here and helpin' Charley and Francine. Roy's a big boy. He can drive that big ole motor home on his own. He's had plenty of experience driving it while on tour. Jimmy can take Julia on back. I'll stay as long as I'm needed. It's been a pleasure with you all."

"Thank you for that, Minnie Pearl." I said. "Thank you all. You are all so wonderful. So wonderful…You have no idea how much Charley and I appreciate all of you coming here. You made Charley's dream come true. My dream has come true." I started to choke up. "Minnie, you are welcome here forever. Stay as long as you want. It's true, we'll need your help." I squeezed Charley's hand. "I appreciate your offer."

"Hey, hey, let's not forget why I came over. Lighten up, it's starting to feel like a funeral around here. We've got some happy talk to go over." Lou said. "I tell you what, yesterday was trying but extremely gratifying. I was really moved by Elsie Swanson."

"You mean the elderly lady with the fried pies?" Julia asked.

"Yes. That was really touching. Can you imagine making prize winning pies and forgetting about it? She still had the unconscious ability to make those pies and she did, but she couldn't remember doing it. Amazing. During the awards ceremony, she and her daughter sat stoically in the front row. I was watching them the whole time I was emceeing. The old lady sat motionless. I remember her now. Hadn't seen her in years."

"What was her name again? Was it Danise? Danise Childress? Wow. What a remarkable woman that daughter is. Wonderful. Talking to her so sweetly and helping her up to the stage for her award. I don't think I'll ever forget it." Irma said.

Lou moved to a vacant chair next to Charley. "Looky here, Charley." Lou opened Charley's day planner. "I spent most of last night and this morning crunching numbers. Do you understand this?" He pointed to the day planner and moved his finger from the left column descriptions and the right column numbers. Charley grunted in agreement and tried to shake his head up and down. I looked over their shoulders and saw the impressive numbers. The town had turned quite a profit. I was amazed at the success. The best window I looked through now, was not the book, however, it was seeing that Charley's brain had the ability of reading and comprehension. He understood what we talked about. My spirit lifted.

22

IT'S BEEN NEARLY SIX WEEKS since the Prickleberry Pie Contest took place. James, Julia, Irma and Roy have gone home. Minnie Pearl has stayed on and works with Charley during the day. She's become his personal nurse. I've come to believe that she has some healing powers. He's shown such progress. I feel guilty that she's been here this long, however, she has been the greatest help and asset I have right now. Another couple of weeks and she'll go home. He'll be all mine.

Pamela and I are still running the shop together. Charley will join us as his therapy schedule warrants. He still hasn't been to the shop since he returned. It's been too difficult to maneuver him in his wheelchair. While it will be some time before he can resume his store activities, his progress shows that there is a lot of potential to eventually resume it. We need to be slow and steady.

I opened the store early today. Business has picked up since the pie contest. It's hard to keep up. Pamela and I need a helper. It will be great when Charley can resume some of his duties.

"Hello, dear!" Pamela yelled as she entered the store. "Look what I brought in." She said as she flipped her blue ribbon back and forth. "Here's my First Prize for my custard pie. I'm going to hang it on the wall there." She pointed to the spot where she intended to put it.

"That's great, Pamela. I'm so proud of you!" What I want to know is when are you going to make me and Charley the prize-winning pie? I've yet to taste it."

"Oh darling, I know. We've been so busy. It's hard to bake when I get home. I just don't seem to have the time anymore."

"Could you give up your recipe? Why couldn't we make a few of your custard pies and sell them? We could advertise them as first place awardwinning."

"That's a great idea, Francine. I don't know why I didn't think of it."

"Great. Bring it in tomorrow. We'll make some time this week. Hey, did I tell you that Ruta Mae called me last night? Remember that Tim Clary from Peregrine Publishing? The fellow that worked on the cookbook?"

"Yes, the guy I wanted to punch in the nose?" Her blue English eyes were twinkling, so gleefully.

"One and the same. Well, Ruta and he have been dating since the contest.

He just asked her to go steady. She said yes. She really likes him."

"Well, I hope he doesn't treat her rudely. She's only dated him for what, six weeks? It's too soon to go steady." Pamela's voice sounded proper with authority.

"Oh Pamela! You're so funny. Always caring in the old school way." I grabbed her and put my arm around her waist giving her a squeeze. "Have I told you how much I care about you? You're my best friend."

"I love you too, Francine. I'll always be your friend. You mean the world to me. Plus I need the job."

"You're such a card!"

"Queen of Hearts, my dear."

I looked out the window and saw Lou approaching the door. Then he stopped outside with a huge grin on his face. I turned away as I placed a tray of cookies in the display case. As I straightened up, I looked again at the door. I had expected Lou to walk in already. Lou opened the door and stepped in, holding the door open.

"Hey, I see Pamela has nailed up her First Prize Blue Ribbon." Lou announced.

"Yes, she has. She just put it up this morning. I've been after her to make me her famous custard pie. Maybe this week we'll make a couple together. Did you taste the prize winning pie at the contest?"

"No, I didn't get the chance. I had to focus on emceeing the festivities. That reminds me, though."

"Reminds you what?"

Just then, Lou's arm still resting on the door handle, moved aside keeping the door open. A figure slowly edged towards the door opening. I turned and looked. Charley was standing in the doorway, balancing with his cane. Minnie Pearl was standing behind him, grinning from ear to ear.

"Welcome Home, Charley!" Everyone yelled simultaneously.

"One more thing," Lou said, "before you start this great day… the People's Choice Award still has not been given. We're still counting the votes that everyone submitted from the public pie tasting. I'd like to grant the award soon. Actually, I think we should give Charley the honor. This was his project, wasn't it, Big C? Wotcha, think?"

A broad smile radiated from Charley's face.

"If you've tried the pies and picked a favorite, did you submit your vote yet?"

23

THINGS ARE SLOWLY RETURNING TO normal. Charley is progressing better than expected. Brain damage is a wicked affliction. It treats everyone differently. We've learned to tackle one issue at a time. One day a week is speech therapy, the next day may be coordination or physical movement. By the end of the week, we have covered the problem areas and will start over on Monday. Week after week it continues. Very draining for a caregiver but contrarily every little improvement boosts the morale.

On this early spring evening, I decided to wheel Charley down to the square.

It is easier and quicker for me in handling him. One day soon, he will be able to walk on his own. It's dark outside and with a slight breeze, it feels more cold than cool. I park him next to my favorite bench. The lighting makes it feel romantic. We hold hands.

"Charley, I want you to know that I love it here. You made the best choice for us. We've done good." I smile at him. He cracks a smile as well. "I want to show you something. I noticed it today and I couldn't wait to share it with you."

I point my other hand forward towards the sidewalk, on the side of the square facing our store. Someone had cut out a half-moon planter about twelve feet from tip to tip. It was planted with daffodils that were now in bloom. It was a beautiful crescent of sunny yellow happy daffodils.

"Look!' I said. "They have found us. My little joy of spring that blew away. They are back. You are back. Welcome Home!"

ABOUT THE AUTHOR

Karen Ganger, her husband, and little dog, Dinks, divide their home time between a picturesque 133 acre wooded retreat in the Ozark Mountains and a home on Puget Sound, in the shadow of Mt. Rainier, near Seattle. A retired Casualty Claims Manager, she currently works part-time as an archivist preserving documents. Karen has an interest in preserving traditional ethnic recipes, having collected and archived them for over fifty years. She is an avid cook, traveler, and gardener.

www.ingramcontent.com/pod-product-compliance
Ingram Content Group UK Ltd.
Pitfield, Milton Keynes, MK11 3LW, UK
UKHW022227230426